KT-481-545

the SEVENTEEN SECRETS of the KARMa CLUB

Karen McCombie's Scrumptious Books

Happiness, and All That Stuff

Deep Joy, or Something Like It

Collect all 16 fabulous titles!

A Guided Tour of Ally's World

My V. Groovy Ally's World Journal

7 sunshiney, seasidey unmissable books

And her novels

Marshmallow Magic and the Wild Rose Rouge

An Urgent Message of Wowness

the seventeen secrets of the karma club

KAREN McCOMBIE

SCHOLASTIC

Scholastic Children's Books
An imprint of Scholastic Ltd
Euston House, 24 Eversholt Street
London, NW1 1DB, UK
Registered office: Westfield Road, Southam, Warwickshire, CV47 0RA
SCHOLASTIC and associated logos are trademarks and or registered trademarks of
Scholastic Inc.

Text copyright © Karen McCombie
The right of Karen McCombie to be identified as the author of this work
has been asserted by her.

ISBN 978 1407 10516 1

A CIP catalogue record for this book
is available from the British Library

All rights reserved
This book is sold subject to the condition that it shall not,
by way of trade or otherwise, be lent, hired out or otherwise circulated in any
form of binding or cover other than that in which it is published. No part of this
publication may be reproduced, stored in a retrieval system, or transmitted in any
form or by any means (electronic, mechanical, photocopying, recording
or otherwise) without the prior written permission of
Scholastic Limited.

Printed by GGP Media GmbH, Poessneck
Papers used by Scholastic Children's Books are made from wood grown in
sustainable forests.

1 3 5 7 9 10 8 6 4 2

This is a work of fiction. Names, characters, places, incidents
and dialogues are products of the author's imagination or are used fictitiously.
Any resemblance to actual people, living or dead, events or locales is
entirely coincidental.

www.scholastic.co.uk/zone

CAMDEN LIBRARIES	
4332965 4	
JB	BIB
24-Jun-2009	PETERS
£7.99	

For Bel Cowie,
though we never did meet. . .

Contents

The Colour of Secrets

I feel things in colour.

Chunks of my life, I mean.

When I think of being little, it's all hazy light blue. I guess it's hazy 'cause you can't quite remember stuff from a time when you were so small that pigeons seemed as big as velociraptors. And maybe it's light blue 'cause I hung out a lot in my buggy back then, staring up at the sky and spotting clouds that looked like teddy bears and ducks and rice cakes.

Silver: that's the colour that flashes into my head when I remember the speed and excitement of taking a wrong turn and hurtling down the hilly path in our local park the day (aged four-and-nearly-a-quarter) I got my stabilizers taken off. I wasn't scared – just thrilled. (My dad, Neil, wasn't scared either – well, not for *me*. Just absolutely terrified of taking me back home to Mum in *bits*. . .)

The summer I was seven seems all lemon yellow and bright white and aubergine purple. We were only in Greece for two weeks, but in my mind, the fruit on the trees and the boxy, bleached houses seeped right through my entire holidays that year, same as the mammoth bruises I got on both knees from tripping over an inflatable shark round the hotel pool.

Then there's a flash of tropical orange for the time I

got a part in the school play (aged nine) and had to act as the narrator, standing in a beam of spotlight at the side of the stage, fluffing my lines and gulping a lot.

My tenth birthday party; that was deep blush pink, for sure. It was all down to the fact that my mum, Bibi, is this mad crazy knitting fiend. It's not like she knits neat little pastel cardies for babies in front of the telly of an evening, granny-style. Oh no; she's like the punk goddess of knitting. The cushions on our sofa are all knitted – with mad patterns of goldfish and parrots and tarantulas. There're knitted pictures on the wall (a kind of squint copy of da Vinci's *Mona Lisa*, and a wonky but cute silhouette with a crown, and "God Save The Queen" written under it – in knitted letters, of course). When I was little, she knitted jeans and combat trousers and tiny funky T-shirts for my dolls. When I got older, she knitted me a knee-length black nightdress with a pirate skull and crossbones on it.

But for my tenth birthday party, she really went for it. Me and my friends weren't allowed in the living room till Mum said the word, and when we did go in – starving and desperate for party food – we found it all right, and every bit of it was knitted. Knitted nachos, knitted sandwiches, knitted pizza, knitted jelly and ice cream – even a knitted birthday cake, with wibbly-wobbly knitted candles.

Everyone wowed and oohed a lot, as I blushed pink. The blushing was 'cause I was half stupidly proud of my marginally mental mum and half stupidly embarrassed. I was specially embarrassed when my best friend, Tara, whispered, "Yeah, but there is *real* food too, right?"

2

in that not-good-at-whispering voice that she does. Of course, there *was* real food, which we had after I opened my present from Mum and Dad (Rollerblades wrapped in knitted metallic mohair wool "paper", tied with a knitted red ribbon).

Speaking about Tara . . . it's all lime green and lavender when I think of the years we were best friends. Lime green for all the chatting and gossiping we did; lavender for all the lazing around watching endless DVDs set in American high schools. (Tara could do a mean impression of the typical *mean* American teen queen there always is in those movies.)

But there've been no rainbow colours lately. Not for the last eight or nine months, since Tara's parents decided to switch schools and send her to Brookfield, a bus ride away.

I think Mum saw it coming . . . she tried to gently mention that me and Tara might *gradually* drift apart, in time, when we started hanging out with new people at school.

But you know something? It didn't happen that way; the gradual drifting apart in time, I mean. Blam – it happened almost straight away, with Tara talking non-stop about someone called Robyn, and being "too busy" anytime I suggested getting together. And the business about hanging out with new people didn't really happen for me either. Yeah, I could dip into stuff with Amira and her crew, or chat at breaktimes to Mel or Lily or Shannon or whoever, but there wasn't a Robyn for *me*.

And so the last few months had been a bit, well, *beige*. Which is an absolutely OK colour for porridge and hamster bedding and dried-in mud. It's just that it's not exactly the most amazing colour for your *life*.

Still, you never can tell what's around the corner.

And round *my* particular corner, something unexpected was heading my way: secrets. A whole bunch of 'em. *Seventeen* of them, to be precise.

But not *all* of them were going to be in glorious technicolour. A few were destined to be thundery grey, for sure. . .

The First Secret

The Karma Club.

It all began with the old lady getting splatted by the bike.

Or maybe it didn't; maybe it all started when the newsagent was moaning (as usual) about the homeless guy selling the charity newspaper outside his shop.

Or maybe it started because of Mum buying mints from the newsagent, which she did 'cause she thought it might stop her feeling suddenly sick.

Which means maybe it really started with Scarlet, but perhaps that's going *too* far back. . .

Let's just start in the newsagent.

"Your special magazine is here early," said Mr Patel, pulling something out from under the counter, as Mum rattled through the coins in her knitted ladybird purse to pay for the mints.

At Mr Patel's secretive-sounding words, an elderly lady rifling amongst the biscuits glanced through her mauve-framed glasses with a frown, probably expecting to see some dodgy-looking bloke buying a horribly tacky magazine featuring big-boobed women wearing very few clothes. Instead, she seemed surprised to spy my very eye-catching mum smiling happily at the sight of her favourite knitting magazine.

The old lady let her eyes roam up and down the vision of Mum: from long, light brown, tangly hair pinned up with knitted flower hairslides, to the large sunflower tattoo on her arm, past the big bump of her belly straining against her T-shirt dress (my baby sister, due in eight weeks), to the knitted spangly laces in her trainers.

She stopped staring when she noticed a plain-looking thirteen-year-old girl in jeans, stripy T-shirt and long plaits staring straight back at her. (Yep, *me*. I *know* my mum is very hard to miss, but I just don't like it if people ogle her as if she's a piece of experimental street theatre.)

The old lady coughed a little and went back to comparing the price of biscuits, though her face was still a little screwed up in disapproval, which was pretty funny, actually, as Mum's day job – seeing as how being the punk goddess of knitting didn't pay any bills – was occupational therapy, specializing in the elderly.

"Oh, thanks, Mr Patel!" Mum said with a smile, digging more money out of her purse. "I'm just on my way to my knitting group now. I'll pass this around for a bit of inspiration!"

"Look! Look at that!" said Mr Patel, glad of an audience as he glowered at the figure standing outside his shop window. "Someone buying from him again! They buy a magazine from him – they don't come in here to buy from *me*! He is taking my trade!!"

Mr Patel was so wrapped up in grouchiness that he didn't seem to hear anything from the back of the shop – but me and Mum did. It was only a small sound;

a sort of tut, followed by a long sigh. Poor Mrs Patel . . . she probably understood as well as we did that people bought a copy of *The Big Issue* from the homeless guy outside because he was, well, *homeless*. It didn't mean that it would stop them from coming in the shop to get a newspaper or a packet of crisps or a travel pass or whatever.

But try telling that to Mr Patel. He went on about the *Big Issue* seller to every customer who came into the shop. I bet he said it to little kids trundling in for their Chocolate Buttons and *Thomas The Tank Engine* comics. His wife must have been sick to death of hearing the same old moan.

"Maybe Mrs Patel should buy herself some earplugs," I suggested once we were safely outside, helping myself to a mint from the packet Mum was holding out.

"I could knit her some earmuffs!" Mum said with a grin. "Here, Kezzy . . . nip back and get us a copy of *The Big Issue*. And you know what to do with the change, right?"

Of course I did.

Sneaking a peek in the shop, I saw that Mr Patel was busy with the old lady and her biscuit selection. So I quickly hurried back to the *Big Issue* bloke and held out my money.

"BARK! BARK! BARK! BARK! BARK!"

Grrr. Right next door to the newsagent was the Parade Café, with tables outside. And tied round the leg of one chair was an ugly, barky dog, who *might* just draw Mr Patel's attention to me, if I wasn't careful. It was smallish and squareish, with mean little black eyes aimed my way like a radar, as if it was ready to fire itself straight at me if not for the lead holding it back. Its spiky brownish fur was as strokeable as a toilet brush. Its snaggly bottom teeth jutted out, practically touching its nose with every bark. And there were *plenty* of barks.

"BARK! BARK! BARK! BARK! BARK!"

"Shush!" I hissed at it.

I sort of knew the ugly, barky dog. He lived further along my road with a bland-looking bald guy who never seemed to notice that his dog was both ugly and barky. What I knew from passing its garden gate a million times was that the Ugly Barky Dog didn't *ever* stop barking for *anything*, so I guess I was wasting my shushes.

"BARK! BARK! BARK! BARK! BARK!"

"Can I have a copy, please?" I asked the *Big Issue* bloke quickly, before Mr Patel spotted me and banned me from his shop for ever for consorting with the enemy. (And where would I get my magazines and packets of Hula Hoops after school then?)

"Ta, love," the *Big Issue* bloke smiled, showing a set of teeth that could have done with a wash and brush-up from a dental hygienist. Still, when you're homeless, having a pearly-white smile is probably pretty low on your list of priorities. "Here's your copy, and I'll just get your change. . ."

His name was Glen, I suddenly noticed, catching sight of his pinned-on name tag with the *Big Issue* logo above it. My noticing took a microsecond, and in another microsecond I was gone, following Mum through a gap in the traffic before Glen got a chance to hand me any coins back.

"Thanks, love!" we heard him call out above the traffic's roar and the non-stop barking. As we got to the other side of the pavement, me and Mum turned and gave Glen a wave.

From this distance, he suddenly looked the pale watery blue of an ice cube. That wasn't anything to do with the colour of his skin, or the red T-shirt he was wearing, or his denim jacket and jeans. It was the colour he seemed to be: the colour of cold, like he could never warm up, even on a sunny day like today. In the same way, Mr Patel was the deep vivid red of anger, as his face appeared behind the glass of his shop window and shot dark looks at Glen and his bundle of magazines.

"Not a cloud in the sky," said Mum, staring upwards, as we left the pavement and headed into the park. "We'll set up outside today!"

Mum ran this knitting group that met up at eleven o'clock at the park café every Saturday morning. She'd been doing it for about two years, and was proud of her knitting buddies, who came in as many shapes, sizes and colours as the knitted stuff they made. She had a poster on the café notice board, with a lacy, knitted border around it, in neon pink Lurex thread. It said *Love knitting? Not ashamed who knows it? Then join the Rebel Knitters' Society!* When she'd been trying to come up with a name, Dad had said, "Why don't you call yourselves the Knitting Nutters?" His head was targeted with three balls of cotton-mix wool in a row for that. . .

"Mum, let *me*," I ordered her, five minutes later, as I caught her trying to drag a table from inside the café through the large folding doors to the patio area outside. The knitters would have the sun on their backs and the smell of rose bushes to inspire them, as well as occasional splashes from the little kids lolloping around in the paddling pool beside us. "*I'll* sort the tables and the chairs – *you* get the juice and stuff."

"Thanks, Kezzy, honey," said Mum, straightening herself up gingerly, as if she were surprised to find how tough it was to manoeuvre large pieces of furniture when you're in possession of a very large bump. But then, being pregnant again so long after having me was pretty much a surprise all round to my mum and dad – and *me*, of course. After thirteen years of having my parents to myself, it was strange to think of a new, small girly person muscling in. Not that I minded the muscling in too much. I just hoped the new small girly person wouldn't mind wearing the knitted tomato baby hat which was Mum's latest project. . .

It was heavier than it looked – the long, metal-legged table, I mean – and I could feel my face flushing an attractive shade of red as I huffed and puffed it into position. I glanced up and into the café, checking that Mum wasn't watching me struggling. Nope – she was laughing and chatting with the woman at the counter. But someone *else* was watching . . . someone with a Cornetto in her hand, waiting patiently to pay, and passing the time by staring at me.

I knew her, I realized with a start. Well, *sort* of knew her. Her name was Nell Smith; she'd only joined my class at the beginning of this week. She seemed a bit quiet, but then you *would* be, if you'd just started a new school. I hadn't talked to her yet, mainly 'cause Leanne and Aimee and their crew had sort of swept her up like she was their new pet or something.

Two weeks with them and she'd be spouting bitchy comments about anyone that came within a ten-kilometre radius of her, same as Leanne and Aimee did. I probably never *would* get to know Nell Smith very well, or *want* to. I certainly didn't want to be stared at right now, and gave her a look that said so. Good – she got the message and dropped her gaze to the glazed tile floor of the café straight away.

Er, nope – she was looking back up again and sort of *grinning*.

Great. . .

"All right, Kezzy?" a voice surprised me.

Clunk went the leg of the table on my trainer. Crunch went one of the fifty-two bones that are in the average foot.

"Uh . . . hi!" I said, trying to sound as if I wasn't in pain. Why did I need to pretend this in front of my ex-best friend and her new best friend? I didn't know. I guess I just needed to seem as normal and non-pathetic as possible.

"Uh, what're you *doing*?" asked Tara, arching her eyebrows at me. Wow – she'd plucked them! And I could see that she'd been growing her dark bob out. It was *just* long enough now to be scraped back into a casually messy ponytail, same as Robyn's lighter brown version.

Robyn's mouth was slightly tilted up at the corners, but if that was meant to represent a smile, it wasn't working too well for her. Fantastic – more staring. Robyn was eyeing up my long, blondy-brown plaits. She didn't get that I wore my hair that way 'cause I just liked it, and thought it was kind of funky, specially with the cute jewelled hairclips I wore at the sides. Robyn thought it was a five-year-old's hairdo, but she didn't need to say it in words – her eyes and her sneer said it *way* loud enough.

"I'm helping Mum set up for her club," I told Tara, wondering why I needed to remind her about it, since helping Mum set up was what I'd done – what *she'd* sometimes helped do – every Saturday morning over the last couple of years.

"Oh, yeah, the *knitting* club!" said Tara, sarcasm *dripping* from the word "knitting". I knew she'd always thought Mum's hobby was a bit ditzy, but I hadn't realized she'd shifted her opinion from "ditzy" to "naff".

What had changed Tara so much? I wondered, as my face pulsed pink and my foot throbbed pain. Was it just changing schools? Was it changing best friends? I was totally confused. I mean, was this the *real* Tara, and the person who'd seemed to be my best mate just an act? Or was Robyn some kind of witch (quite possibly, by the look of that sneer) who'd magicked away the nice, normal Tara and put a changeling in her place?

"Omigod – that is *well* huge!" Tara suddenly exclaimed, staring in vague horror at something behind me.

I knew before I turned round that she was talking about my mum. Talking about her like she'd morphed into a humpback whale or something, instead of a person who was very, very pregnant and totally chilled out about it.

Oblivious, Mum was laughing to herself. She was holding up a pink plastic pitcher of juice, grinning as she tried to see past her bump and pad her way down the three steps that led out of the café. Her T-shirt dress was excellent, I thought proudly. It was bright green, with a big yellow smiley face stretched bizarrely over the bump.

"Urgh, *gr*—"

Robyn stopped herself. But I knew the word that had nearly popped out was "gross". A swell of anger started to rise in my chest – but a sudden blur of movement and noise stopped me in my tracks.

(I didn't know it right *then*, but the First Secret was about one minute away.)

The noise part of the blur: it was a jumble of kiddy yelps, squealing bike tyres, a shocked "Oh!" followed by a thump, followed by low groans.

The movement part of the blur: it consisted of a teenage boy on his bike, hurtling past the "NO CYCLING" signs at high speed, skidding to avoid a now-sobbing toddler, and smashing instead into an old lady who fell sprawling on the ground, holding a wrist which was visibly – even from here – dangling at a *very* peculiar angle.

"Pfffffffffffft!" snorted Robyn, as if she were sniggering at some dumb, knockabout scene from *The Simpsons*.

"Did you see that? It was like – like she was one of those pin things getting knocked down in a bowling alley!"

Tara's comment wasn't worth listening to, and I only just heard it as I started racing towards the old lady, beating my mum to her by a millisecond. And right behind my mum, chucking her Cornetto into the bushes as she crouched down to help, was Nell Smith.

"Don't move her!" Mum ordered both of us, as Nell Smith and I went to slip a hand each under the old lady's arms and help her up.

Next there came more blurs, of faces all around, stopped to stare uselessly in shock (apart from the blur of a bike hurtling out of the far gate). The next blur involved a volley of words, as Mum fired questions and orders.

"How do you feel? What hurts? Can you try to gently move your hand for me?" (To the shocked old lady, who was still clinging on to a shopping bag with her good hand, though its contents – a small carton of milk and a packet of biscuits – had been flung halfway to the paddling pool.)

"Can you go to the café and ask for some ice, and maybe a tea towel to help get the swelling down?" (To Nell Smith, who nodded, happy to help.)

"And Kezzy – catch. Call 999 and ask for an ambulance." (To me, as her silver flip-top phone came hurtling through the air my way.)

Thinking back, I guess it was a bright white moment, a moment that plays out now in slow motion in my head.

We both started to rise at the same time, me and Nell Smith, then noticed something on the tarmac ground and swooped to get it, our fingers nearly interlacing around the mauve-framed specs that had fallen from the old lady's face when she fell.

Our eyes met, mine and Nell Smith's, and it was the strangest feeling: as if we both suddenly felt we knew something very strongly, only we hadn't figured out *what* exactly.

We didn't know it then – in that bright white moment – but the First Secret of the Karma Club was this: that it was about to exist.

And me and Nell Smith were going to be its first and *only* members. . .

The Second Secret

Nell Smith: all floppy dark curls, brown eyes and olive skin. But still, to me, she seemed the blinding, bright white of a sheet flapping in the wind on a sunny day.

Would she *like* being compared to a sheet? *Probably not*, I thought, keeping my dumb technicolour thoughts to myself. . .

"Go on – *your* turn!" said Nell, nudging me into doing a good deed.

I glanced around, wondering what sort of good deed to do. Hold on – I suddenly had an idea. I had crisps . . . and all I had to do was offer one to the nearest kid. That could work! And the nearest kid happened to be this little boy, standing hesitantly by the side of the paddling pool, wearing swim shorts with cartoon sharks on and with a thumb wedged in his mouth.

"Hey, want a crisp?" I asked, lunging forward and getting down on my knees beside him (*ouch*, my crunched foot). He was about two, or maybe three. I'm not too hot at figuring out little kids' ages.

But however old he actually was, my good deed fell flat as a clown tripping over his oversized shoes in a circus ring.

"*Wahhhhhhhhh!!!*" howled the kid, taking his thumb out of his mouth long enough to let it be known that my crispy act of kindness was as welcome as a migraine.

He probably thought I was the sort of "strange" stranger his mother had warned him about.

"*That* went well!" I muttered, grinning self-consciously, and sitting myself back down on the bench beside Nell as quickly as I could. So much for my best attempt at a spontaneous good deed.

"Y'know, *he* was the kid who nearly got run over by the bike," Nell pointed out, as the toddler ran off to find his mum amongst the scrum of parents and kids hanging out around the park café and paddling pool.

I guess that made me feel a tiny bit better, and a tiny bit less stupid. His two- (or three-?) year-old nerves were probably jangled, which was why he'd reacted so badly to my offer of a free crisp. (Yeah, *that* and the stranger-danger factor.)

"And *I* didn't have much luck either, did I?" smiled Nell.

Nope, she hadn't. Her attempt at a good deed had been to jump up and hand a pretty peach rose to a passing old man who was leaning heavily on his walking stick.

The old dude wasn't so much charmed at the kind gesture as *furious*. "You *can't* go picking flowers off the bushes! That's park property, that is!" he'd scolded her, too deaf or too annoyed by the youth of today to hear Nell stutteringly explain that it was broken off and lying on the ground already.

Actually, there were quite a lot of leaves and sticks and petals scattered on the ground; one of the two burly ambulance men who'd come to the old lady's rescue an hour ago had found it hard to squeeze himself and his first-aid bag into the space between the shrubs and

Audrey (Mrs Audrey Hooper, in fact: Mum had got her name out of her between gasps of pain and panic).

But hey – what a difference an hour could make. Hopefully Audrey would be feeling a lot better now that she and her wrist were being cared for at the hospital, and Mum was certainly more relaxed, swapping her Florence Nightingale role for the non-exhausting job of chatting and click-clacking with her fellow rebel knitters at the big table by the café's French doors.

And *I* was having a deeply unexpected and hugely fun time with someone who bizarrely appeared to be (perhaps, fingers crossed) my new best friend. . .

After waving Audrey off into the ambulance, we'd hovered – me and Nell Smith – all awkward and shy, till Helen, the woman who ran the café, came running out with two free Cornettos for us. "Payment for helping out there – well done!" she'd smiled at us.

I guess me and Nell had thawed over freezing strawberry-flavoured ice creams, and found out some random stuff about each other. And here's a random selection of some of that random stuff:

- Nell liked Magnums better than Cornettos, but they'd run out in the café freezer. I told her I was kind of partial to a Twister myself.
- I explained that the very nice but slightly nutty-looking pregnant lady with the sunflower tattoo on her arm was my mum. *She* said she wished her mum dressed more like mine, and less like a walking advert for a hiking company.
- She didn't much like Leanne and Aimee in our

class and was figuring out how to un-adopt herself from them without seeming rude. I told her they'd bitch about her no matter what, so she should just get away from them as quickly as possible and not stress about being rude.

- Her family had just moved from Manchester, but she'd lived all over the country, like in Cardiff and Aberdeen and some place or *couple* of places else (I forget). I asked if her dad was a criminal on the run or something, and she laughed (phew), and said no – he was a big-shot manager of a big chain of whatevers (I forget, *again*) and kept getting moved by his firm. I told her that *my* dad used to be a manager too, but swapped the kitchen warehouse he slogged his guts out in for a nursery (one with kids, not plants). She laughed, but not in a nasty, "Wait: your *dad* is, like, a *nursery* teacher?!" kind of a way. (Unlike some – OK, *most* – people did.)
- Her favourite clothes shop was H&M (she didn't tell me that – I recognized everything she was wearing from drooling around the local branch about ten million times).
- She told me she was an only child. I told *her* I had a bump of a sister coming soon. She giggled and said she'd kind of noticed already.
- Her old best mate was called Neve, and had promised to email her every day, but had only emailed once, with a message that said, *"How are you? Can't write much now, going out. Will*

get back to you later today. . ." (that was six days ago). *I* told *her* that my best mate was the girl who'd been sniggering beside me when the old lady had been knocked over by the hit-and-run jerk on the bike. (Who knew – or much cared – where Tara had disappeared to since.)

- She thought our black and yellow school uniform was v.v. bad. I said, "What, don't you *like* looking like a bee?!"
- She particularly liked:
  a) her name (though not when dumb boys sang "Nelly The Elephant")
  b) happy hip-hop (i.e., not the stuff that mentioned guns or bling, or called girls rude names)
  c) Irn Bru (the fizzy drink from Scotland), and . . .
  d) cute and dippy films (examples – *Little Miss Sunshine* and *Amelie*).
- *I* told *her* that:
  a) I didn't know anyone else called Nell (which made her name pretty cool to me)
  b) I didn't know any hip-hop stuff that didn't feature guns or bling, or girls being called rude names (but would be interested in hearing some)
  c) I hadn't ever tasted Irn Bru, but I tried root beer once and barfed, and . . .
  d) my favourite film in the whole world happened to be *Amelie*.

We'd got a bit over-excited talking about *Amelie*, in a way that I never got excited talking about the American high school movies I'd always watched with Tara. But that was maybe because the American high school movies had much the same plot every single time (a heroine disliked by the nasty cheerleaders, a supposedly cute boy, a baseball game and a high school prom). But not many films had a plot involving an adorable French girl who did (mostly) good deeds as a hobby, and fell in love with a guy who collected dropped snaps from passport photo booths in train stations. . .

And yep, wittering on about the movie got us both coming over all Amelie and trying out a couple of good deeds ourselves. Pity they hadn't had a movie-style reaction.

"Maybe good deeds are too much like hard work," I mumbled, crunching a large curl of cheesy Quaver. "We helped that old lady – maybe we should just stop there."

"Nah . . . my dad always says karma loves a trier!" said Nell, scrunching up her own now-empty crisp bag (the second course of our non-nutritious post-rescue snack).

"Your dad says *what*?" I asked, understanding not a word of what Nell had just said.

"Well, Dad likes fooling around with phrases and sayings. So the phrase should be 'God loves a trier', but he changed it to karma. Sorry – it kind of makes sense, in *my* house at least."

My forehead was still scrunched in confusion. It probably wasn't that flattering a look.

"Karma: as in you do *bad* stuff, and *bad* stuff happens to you . . ." I tried.

". . . and if you do good stuff, then etc, etc. Yep, that's about it," nodded Nell. "So Dad sort of means the good karma part. Like you should always at least *try* to do nice stuff."

"I s'pose," I answered, thinking that most of the time me, Mum and Dad tried to be nice to other people, ourselves and each other. I say *most* of the time, 'cause sometimes it was hard to feel all warm and glowy when Mum was nagging me to tidy my room, or Dad had eaten *all* the biscuits (as usual) or Leanne and Aimee and their mates were sniggering at me for *marginally* mispronouncing something in French class or blinking a funny way or whatever.

Leanne and Aimee . . . they must have a bunch of bad karma coming their way, for sure, the way they niggled and narked. And plenty of other people I knew of too, come to think of it, like Mr Patel, since he spent an awful lot of time uselessly whingeing on about the *Big Issue* bloke. Then there was a mum who'd moved into the house across the street a couple of months ago . . . she seemed to be taking care of a *herd* of small kids on her own, and must've been going for the Most Harassed Single Mum in Britain Award, by the scowly look on her face and grouch in her voice when she spoke to (OK, *barked* at) her brood. When I watched her out of my bedroom window last week, I realized I'd never once seen her smile. Maybe *that* was karma; be ratty to your kids too much and your face will end up permanently looking like you just bit into a slug sandwich.

"*I* know! We need a notebook!!" said Nell, plonking her flip-flops on the ground and standing up. "That shop over there . . . that should have one, shouldn't it?"

Nell almost looked like Amelie for a second; all wide eyes and enthusiastic expression. Well, only the wide eyes and enthusiastic expression really reminded me of Amelie, since Nell had dark brown, floppy curls instead of a sharp bob, and was kind of curvier than the straight-up-and-down actress we both knew and adored.

"Uh, yes," I replied, thinking about the couple of stationery shelves at the back of Mr Patel's shop, just across the road from the park entrance Nell was pointing to. "Um . . . what do we need a notebook for, exactly?"

"To write all our good deeds down in!" Nell said assuredly, walking towards the main park path.

"OK. . ."

I followed, giving Mum a quick wave and an elaborate mime about going to the shop and being back in two minutes.

This was quite exciting. Nell obviously assumed we'd be doing at least enough good deeds to fill a few pages of a notebook, which meant that she also obviously assumed we'd be friends, just like that.

I mean, I'd been pretty sure we'd had that odd this-*means*-something moment when we'd both bent down to pick up Audrey's specs from the ground and found ourselves staring at each other, but it was reassuring to realize that I hadn't just made it all up in my feeble brain.

In fact, it felt stomach-squeezingly great to think Nell felt the same way. When we stepped into Mr Patel's shop (with me nipping self-consciously past Glen the *Big Issue* bloke, who was busy serving someone), it was all I could do to stop myself from running over to the spinning stand and buying her a *"Hey, you're my best friend!"* card.

Luckily, I resisted, in case she thought I was a tiny bit mad and changed her mind. . .

"How about this one?" asked Nell, holding up a notepad with stripes on it. It was the sort of thing you'd tear pages out of to leave *"Gone to shops for beans"* messages on. It wasn't nearly special enough.

"Nah," I said, rummaging amongst the large and small, plain and patterned pads. And then I saw it: gold (pretend) satin, edged with genuine (plastic) amber and green jewels. It was dusty and had three price tags on it, stuck one on top of the other, as Mr or Mrs Patel had steadily reduced it, the longer it had lain unbought and unloved. All we needed was 50p and it was ours.

"Absolutely!" said Nell, seizing it from me and marching up to the counter, where Mrs Patel was patiently waiting and smiling. (Maybe Mr Patel had worn himself out with all that frowning at the *Big Issue* bloke and needed a lie-down.)

Three minutes, two straws and one apple juice later, and we were sitting at one of the tables inside the Parade Café, next to the newsagent's. Nell had the first page open and was chewing the end of her pen, thinking.

I was hunkered down opposite her, trying to make myself as small as possible ('cause of someone outside the café window).

"How about . . . 'The Good Deeders'?" Nell suggested, not seeming to notice my hunkering.

We needed a name, she said. For the club we seemed to have invented. We needed to think of one and write it at the front of *our* book, where we were going to record all the little acts of kindness that we were going to do together. We two who were amazingly best friends, just like that. Again, I felt slightly dizzy-brained with happiness, even if I *was* trying to make myself impossibly small and use my new best friend as a human shield ('cause of that someone outside the café window).

"Or 'The Golden Moments Club'?" I threw in, inspired by the metallic sheen of the notepad and the two gold heart brooches that Nell had bought on the spur of the moment from the charity box Mrs Patel had displayed on the counter. A one-pound donation to the British Heart Foundation got you a free heart brooch, which Nell had decided would make a great badge for us both to wear, to show we were members of our un-named society.

The moment I said it, I regretted it. "Golden Moments Club" sounded like a bingo afternoon for the Over-60s.

"No! I've got it!!" Nell burst out. "How about 'The Karma Club'?"

I liked it. Actually I *loved* it, just like I loved everything that had happened in the last hour or so – apart from that old lady Audrey breaking her *wrist,* of course. Maybe karma knew that me and Nell Smith were both OK girls who just needed a break in the best friends department, and had thrown us together with a bang, speeding up the whole getting-to-know-you thing so that a couple of weeks' worth of buddying up and learning to trust each other had happened in, ooh, seventy-five minutes, if my watch was right.

"By the way, why are you sitting like that?" added Nell, changing the subject now that she'd noticed me slithering down in my chair, folding my arms in on myself like a human paper aeroplane.

"You see the guy selling *The Big Issue*?" I whispered over the table, before ducking down while Nell turned around and peered.

"Uh-huh," she said, spinning back to face me. "What about him?"

"I bought a magazine from him earlier, and ran away before he could give me any change. I don't want him to see me, 'cause I don't want him to feel he has to say thank you all over again. That would just be *way* too cringey for *both* of us."

Nell looked straight at me, as if I'd just said something very, very important. And instantly, I understood what she was thinking. We were having another of those weird moments, like we were psychic sisters or twins separated at birth or whatever.

In that very strange moment, we both knew – absolutely – what the *Second* Secret of the newly-named Karma Club would be.

"We're going to do our good deeds –"

"– in secret," I joined in with Nell's sentence.

No one would know. Not the people on the receiving end of our good deeds. Not our closest friends (er, *what* close friends?). Not even our parents, no matter how nice and kooky they might be (yes, I was thinking of my mum in particular).

I grinned. Nell grinned back, as she watched me pin one of the gold hearts on the *inside* collar of my T-shirt.

"Shhh. . ." she said, holding a finger to her mouth, as she pinned her gold heart to the inside of the waistcoat she was wearing.

I winked back, stupidly happy in our conspiracy and desperate to find out what our third secret might be. . .

The Third Secret

"He used to play bass in a sort of punky garage band in Texas."

Texas. Pictures popped into my mind that *must* have been beamed in from telly, since I'd never been there. Texas: vast, endless blue skies; flat, flat fields of golden-yellow corn. Or maybe that was Nebraska. . .

"In Texas? What was he doing *there*?" I asked Nell, trying to match up the big-shot manager dad she'd told me about on Saturday to this sudden image of a grungey guitarist hanging out in America's Deep South(ish).

It was after school on Monday and we were swapping more personal history, me and Nell Smith. At morning break, we'd covered music, films and telly (what we loved, what we loathed); over veggie lasagne in the dining hall at lunch time we'd talked favourite food (Nell: corn on the cob; me: Heinz tomato soup); at afternoon break we'd covered embarrassing childhood crushes (Nell: the spotty paper boy when she'd lived in Cardiff; me: Pingu). The whole time, we were watched by Leanne and Aimee and their mates, silently, with arms folded. You can bet they got the message that Nell didn't want to hang out with them any more. They looked a bit hurt, to tell you the truth, but you can *also* bet they'd started to mull over things they didn't like about her. Whatever. . .

"Dad was getting over a big split with some girlfriend, and he decided to put a pin in a map and go where it took him to get away from everything," said Nell, clutching her hand to her heart and rolling her eyes melodramatically. "The guys he ended up sharing a flat with had a band together, and needed a bass player, so Dad took it up, even though he'd never done it before. He said he was awful – so were the whole band. They used to get beer bottles chucked at them!"

Nell mimed chucking a bottle and then realized she might be spotted and hid behind the postbox with me again.

It wasn't the most normal and relaxed place to have a conversation, but there *was* a point to us being there: we were on a spying mission. The thing is, spying is less glamorous than it sounds: there's a lot of dull hanging around (behind postboxes) to be done, and passing the time with funny stories certainly brightened things up.

Anyway, the story about Nell's dad *was* pretty funny. So was the one I'd just told her about how my parents met. My twenty-two-year-old mum was originally from Leeds, but after a year backpacking on a round-the-world air ticket, she'd found it really hard to settle down when she came back to Britain. So her wunderlust took her to this little surfer-friendly town in Cornwall, where she ended up waitressing in a café. Mum fell in love with local boy Dad when he hobbled into the café one day with half his body covered in cuts and bruises after he rode a wave into an inconveniently large rock. It was a turning point for them both; Dad decided to give up surfing (and crashing), and after taking careful care of her new boyfriend, Mum decided to give up travelling and waitressing and go to university to train to be an occupational therapist so she could help other people.

"I wish Dad had photos from that time," Nell continued, as she peered out from around the side of the postbox, "but he left them – along with lots of other stuff – in a rucksack on a Greyhound bus going to a gig in El Paso."

El Paso . . . that sounded *so* exotic. The place Mum and Dad had met in was a Cornish bay called Wide Mouth.

"OK! This is it!" Nell suddenly blurted out, her gaze fixed on something beyond the postbox. "He's got his back to us – he's talking to someone who's just bought a magazine from him. . ."

"Let's do it!" I announced, glad that I wouldn't have to hold on to the cup of hot chocolate in my hands any more. Burning heat was radiating through the cardboard container and *seriously* melting my fingers.

"*Go!*"

It was a pretty smooth operation.

Step 1: We walked swiftly over to the newsagent's plate glass window, the side nearest Glen and his battered satchel of *Big Issues*.

Step 2: Nell pretended to be fascinated by the small ads in Mr Patel's window: scribbled postcards with the details of cleaners and flute tuition and kittens for sale.

Step 3: With Nell as cover, I hastily bent down and placed the hot chocolate by Glen's bag of mags, making sure the anonymous "*For You, Glen – Have a Nice Day!!*" Post-It note was stuck to the side of it.

Step 4: We moseyed off casually (which actually

turned into running at top speed) past the Parade Café and the shops and round the corner.

Step 5: We leaned against a wall and tried not to die from heart palpitations and lack of oxygen.

"Wish we . . . could see . . . his reaction!" I panted, with a thought suddenly striking me. I'd described Glen to Nell, saying he looked permanently cold, which is why we'd thought that the Third Secret of the Karma Club should involve a cup of hot chocolate (bought from the Parade Café) being "given" to Glen – without him seeing or suspecting us, of course. Only, wouldn't he be *suspicious* of it? I mean, would he think, "How weird, but yum!"? Or "What's the catch? Is there rat poison or washing-up liquid or something in this?" He *must* have seen how Mr Patel scowled in his direction from the safety of his shop window. Glen might worry that it was a way for Mr Patel to be rid of him for ever. . .

"Hey, we *can*!" announced Nell, grabbing the lapel of my blazer and hurtling me across the road, where a number seven bus was idling at a stop.

"But where are we going?" I asked, following her blindly past the driver and up the narrow steep stairs to the top deck, the gold-heart badge pinned to the back of my tie thudding against my ribcage.

A couple of wobbly steps later, as the bus lurched off, we flopped into the nearest double seat.

"Just to the next stop!" Nell answered with a grin. "But this takes us right along the main road – we can see if that Glen guy's drinking it!"

Or pouring the suspected rat poison down the drain, I thought.

But hey, taking a bus one stop to watch a guy pouring suspected rat poison down a drain while struggling to catch my breath was quite an exciting way to pass the time after school on a Monday afternoon. Before Tara switched to Brookfield, the usual amble home would've consisted of us poring over one of Tara's favourite celebrity magazines, doing the "Nice; yuck!; nice; yuck!" thing over every Hollywood starlet and soap actor and their money-no-object, dubious-taste outfits. That could be quite a laugh, only Tara had about *five* favourite celebrity magazines and quite a generous amount of pocket money, so we did it most days, which meant it got to be *not*-so-much of a laugh, for me at least.

"Look, look!" said Nell, squashing a finger up against the glass of the window. I noticed for the first time that she was wearing dark purple varnish (chipped) on her nails (short and bitten). Our form teacher, Miss Lennard, had our class for a lesson first thing tomorrow. She was pretty nice, but pretty hot on school rules. Nail varnish, drop earrings, too much make-up, nuts hairstyles, skirts worn too short, trousers worn too low . . . she'd be on it. I'd better warn Nell. But I'd do it later – first there was a secret mission to assess for success or failure.

"He's drinking it!" I gasped, gazing down at Glen across the street.

"He's reading the note!" squeaked Nell.

"He's smiling!" I added with a broad smile of my own.

We were too loud, we both realized, as a man sitting in front of us turned to see what all the fuss was about.

So a Big Issue *seller is having a drink of coffee or something, while standing on a pavement – so what?* he must've been thinking.

"We did good," said Nell, in a quieter, more conspiratorial voice, as she took the gold notebook and a pen out of her schoolbag. "But we've *got* to be better at being secret next time. He might've seen us when we were running away. . ."

Yeah, or heard us giggling madly with excitement when we were running, I thought, watching as Nell flicked past the page with the details of us helping the old lady, Audrey, at the park on Saturday. Then she flipped the page back.

"D'you realize something?" she said suddenly, almond eyes widening.

"What?" I asked, glancing at the hairy ears of the guy in front, sure he was still listening in, even though we'd taken our conversation down a decibel or two.

"The old lady we helped . . . she was called Audrey, right? Well, that's the name of the actress in *Amelie* – Audrey Tautou! Isn't that amazing?"

For a second, I thought she meant it was amazing that in Britain, Audrey was an un-groovy old-lady name, while it must be pretty funky in France, if the lovely Ms Tautou was anything to go by.

Then, like the soft mauve-y light of dawn, my mind lit up with what Nell was *actually* saying, which was, "Whoooh, spooky coincidence!"

But that wasn't the *spookiest* coincidence of Saturday, I realized with tingling shock, as the mauve dawn in my brain turned to glowing pinky-blue skies.

Audrey (the old lady, not the cool French actress) was in Mr Patel's shop on Saturday morning. *She* had been the person fingering the packets of biscuits while Mum picked up her new knitting magazine! Who'd've guessed that a few minutes after she frowned disapprovingly at my mum, we'd be coming to Audrey's rescue?

I always knew I was allergic to penicillin and eggs. I didn't know I was *also* allergic to an overdose of spooky coincidences.

"Hey . . . your neck's just come out in all these really weird red splatches!" Nell grimaced my way.

I shrunk it down, turtle-style, in the collar of my school shirt, as the man in front proved he *had* been listening and turned to gawp.

It was time to move seats.

"What do you think it means?" I asked Nell, as I finished spilling out the Audrey sighting in Mr Patel's, three seats back on the other side of the bus from our nosy fellow passenger.

Nell was fiesty. Nell was exciting. Nell might have a great answer to this bizarre bit of cosmic craziness.

"Uh, Kezzy – where *are* we. . .?" she asked, worriedly glancing outside the window.

OK, so not everything in me and Nell Smith's lives was destined to be a wondrous, cosmic coincidence.

You can't exactly call being ten stops further on from the place you were supposed to get off at in any way cosmic and wondrous.

Specially knowing there was a long, un-cosmic walk back home. . .

The Fourth Secret

We were being stared at. Hard.

"Hey, isn't . . . isn't *that* the little kid from Saturday?" asked Nell, as the small boy's serious face swung into view and out again. "The one who nearly got splatted by the bike?"

I checked: the boy's face swung into view and out again.

I double-checked, as he swung into view and out again (again).

"Yep, I'm pretty sure it is," I said, even though the kid wasn't either sobbing (like the first time we'd glimpsed him), or wearing swim shorts with cartoon sharks on and running away from me (i.e., the frightening big girl trying to force-feed him Quavers).

He swung around into view again, and I started to feel sick. No offence to the serious little boy – I'm just not too great on roundabouts.

"Can we get off now?" I suggested to Nell.

"Sure. Anyway, I think the evil look we're getting is 'cause the kid wants to come on," said Nell, sticking her red Crocs on the ground and forcing the roundabout to stop in a scuff of rubber.

By the way, Crocs aren't allowed at our school. No slip-on type shoes, on account of Health and Safety regulations, apparently. Can't really figure that one out – maybe the head teacher thinks they'll catch on fire or turn violent or something. And definitely no red shoes; we're allowed a choice between black, blackish black, and very, very dark grey (i.e., black). Being new, Nell probably didn't know all the what-not-to-wear rules (or maybe she'd guessed, but thought she'd try bending them a little to see how far she'd get). Whatever, the normally on-the-ball Miss Lennard seemed oblivious to Nell's dodgy manicure and fire hazard, non-regulation red shoes today (and yesterday, for that matter). She hadn't even noticed that Natty Hunter sat through the whole of her history lesson with a hand over his left ear, listening to Radiohead through one iPod earphone.

The whole hour, Miss Lennard either talked to us in this flat, bored monotone, or stared out of the window grumpily, while we were (supposedly) getting on with our work.

"Do you want a turn?" Nell asked the small boy, who backed away from us wordlessly, as if we'd just asked him to stroke our alligator. ("He's very friendly! He doesn't bite!")

"Some kids are just like that," I said with a shrug, walking away from the roundabout with a slight drunken-looking stagger. "You know how my dad's a nursery nurse?"

"Uh-huh," nodded Nell, ignoring the gate and vaulting over the waist-high playground fence. I wasn't sure I could even negotiate the path properly, after getting travel sick on the roundabout, so I stuck to unlatching the gate.

"He says some kids take practically a whole term just to work up a smile, or get brave enough to ask when they need to go to the loo."

"Yew. Does that mean lots of puddles?" asked Nell.

"I guess so!" I laughed, thinking of the ever-present bucket and mop leaning by the door in Dad's office off the main nursery room.

"What a cool job that must be – apart from the puddles, I mean," said Nell, heading towards the park café on automatic pilot. It was our planned next stop; we were going to spend our Wednesday afternoon mulling over the next secret act of kindness, with an ice cream to help inspire us. "What does your dad do all day – make play-dough sausages and sing nursery rhymes?"

"Yep, that's about it!" I replied, thinking of the occasional days I'd hung out and helped, days when our school had been off for teacher training and of course Mum was at work. It was a lot of fun, reading to the kids or helping them make sand-blobs in the sand pit. (It was *less* fun helping them blow their noses or breaking up toddler fights and ending up getting thunked on the head with dumper trucks for my trouble.)

"I'd rather be *that* kind of teacher than one like Miss Lennard. She's *well* gloomy!" said Nell, talking louder to be heard, now that we were approaching the café and being drowned out by a frantically barking dog tied up outside it. Urgh . . . couldn't I ever escape him? It was bad enough hearing his never-ending yapping on our street, never mind having him disturb my chill-out time in the park. And couldn't he get it through his thick, doggy head that panting with your tongue out and wagging your tail was a better way to make friends than barking fiercely? Any pooch with a smattering of brain cells would figure out that small kids were practically crawling up their mothers' bodies to get *away* from him.

"Miss Lennard's not usually that bad!" I practically shouted back, pulling a scary face at the Ugly Barky Dog, who didn't need to pull a scary face back, having one already. "She's usually pretty interesting. Maybe she's just having a bad day."

"A bad *week*," Nell corrected me, dipping into what felt momentarily like the darkness of the café after the bright, late afternoon sunshine-y light of the park. "We've had two lessons with her, and it's been like getting taught by a gloomy morgue attendant. Actually, you'd probably have more fun in a *morgue* than in our classroom. In a morgue, everyone's dead, so I bet the attendants there put on clown outfits and rollerskate to the radio while no one's looking!"

"So what about your last school – were the teachers better there?" I asked, rifling in the chest freezer for a Twister, but pretty sure at first glance that there weren't any.

"Are you kidding? My old teachers made prison guards seem like tap-dancing children's entertainers!" said Nell, frowning over a serious lack of Magnums, or Cornettos, or anything but Mini Milks, in fact. "Hey, we need to get better ice cream. I can't think properly on just these diddly little things."

Nell held up a tiny, vanilla-flavoured Mini Milk in disgust.

"Well, Mr Patel will probably have some," I suggested, nodding in the direction of the parade of shops just outside the park.

Ping!

At the mention of Mr Patel, inspiration struck, even without the aid of a Twister. . .

Our next good deed – the Fourth Secret of the Karma Club – was lying in a slightly battered envelope on the mat of Mr Patel's shop. Mainly because Nell had just dropped it there.

"Oh!" she exclaimed loudly, picking it up. (As opposed to saying nothing at all when she dropped it, unseen, when we walked in here just now.)

Mr Patel – tap-tapping on his oversized calculator – paused and glanced up distractedly. Mrs Patel, refilling the chocolate bar section on the counter, looked up with a small, enquiring smile.

"Here's some mail for you. . . I just found it on the floor," said Nell, taking the envelope over to the counter.

"But how can this be, at this time?! The postman has already been this morning!" muttered Mr Patel.

"Thank you very much, dear," said Mrs Patel warmly, taking the envelope and studying the front of it.

It was simply addressed to "The Owners of the Newsagent". I was too far away to read it, now that my head was bent over the freezer, but I knew that's what it said because I had written it, about five minutes ago. Just like I'd written the note inside, as Nell dictated it to me.

"Mmm . . . Magnum, great!" said Nell theatrically, coming over to join me and sticking her hand down into the ice vapour escaping from the freezer.

Her eyes were elsewhere, though, same as mine – surreptitiously sneaking a peek at the *Big Issue* bloke's back, as he shuffled from side to side on the pavement beyond the glass of the shop window. Our current good deed was for Mr Patel's benefit, to lower his blood pressure and help him chill out, we hoped. But it would rub off on Glen too, if it worked. And Mrs Patel as well; she'd never have to tut and sigh at her husband's ranting again (till the *next* time he found something or someone to moan about).

The shop suddenly felt very quiet. The clock above the counter tick-tocked, the open freezer hummed and . . . well, that was all, as Mr and Mrs Patel read and digested the letter. The letter which said:

> *To Mr and Mrs Patel (I've heard people call you this in the last few weeks, when I've been standing outside on the pavement),*
>
> *I'm a very, very shy man, so rather than come in and speak to you, I have written you this note to say thank you very much for not complaining about me selling my magazines in front of your shop. I chose to set up my pitch here because it is a busy street, but particularly because your shop is so busy and friendly that a large number of people pass me by on their way in and out, and I have a better chance of selling my magazines and helping myself get enough money to rent a place I can call home.*

*I'm telling you this because at the last place I had
as a pitch, a local shopkeeper ordered me away – he
thought I was trouble, simply because I'm homeless. He
didn't think to understand how difficult my life has been,
and how hard I'm working to get back on my feet.*

*As I say, I'm very shy, so please don't feel you have
to respond to this letter. In fact, I'd like it better if you
acted like you'd never got it.*

All I wanted to say was . . . well, thanks.

Glen (the Big Issue *seller).*

It had taken a couple of scrunched-up attempts to
get the letter right – not the words exactly, more the
writing. The first two looked exactly like they'd been
written by a thirteen-year-old girl (which of course I
am – duh!) but then I'd thought about Dad's spikier
style and tried to channel it on to the paper. The paper
itself was OK – just a lined sheet torn out of a school
pad, and stuffed into an old, plain envelope Nell had
in her bag, which had contained the cheque her mum
had written for school dinners. The sheet of paper and
the scruffy envelope were perfect, though; we didn't
suppose a homeless guy would be expected to have a
pristine floral notelet set or something.

Uh-oh – Mr and Mrs Patel were suddenly talking in
Hindi (I think), so I wasn't sure what they were saying.
But Mr Patel's voice didn't exactly sound sympathetic and
grateful. And Mrs Patel's sounded fast and pleading.

"What does his face look like?" whispered Nell.

I quickly glanced over – and didn't much like what
I saw.

"Red," I muttered out of the corner of my mouth. "Red and angry and . . . oh, no!"

Mr Patel was waving his wife's words away with a careless hand and coming out from behind his counter. Me and Nell straightened up, both clutching our ice lollies for dear life, as he strode past us and out of the shop door with a blee-*bleep*! of the entry alert.

"It's all going to go wrong!" hissed Nell, as our secret good deed seemed about to unravel. If Mr Patel confronted Glen about the letter he'd never written, it was hardly going to make them bond.

"Let's buy these and go. . ." I muttered, turning towards the counter and Mrs Patel. I'd just seen both the men face each other, and couldn't bear to imagine the awkward conversation that was taking place.

"Thank you. . ." Mrs Patel said vaguely, taking the money from us, her eyes fixed on the shop window, at the scene over our shoulders.

Blee-*bleep*!

At the sudden sound of the door, Mrs Patel's hand – laden with our change – took a quick detour and grabbed Glen's letter (ha!) from off the counter, hurriedly shoving it somewhere underneath.

"It's through there, immediately to the right," we heard Mr Patel say, though we were too frozen with fear to turn round. "I was just saying to my wife, that young man can't be standing out there for hours at a time, and have no access to the bathroom. It's not good for one's health. In future, you must not wait to be asked – simply come in, any time."

"Well, thanks – I really appreciate it!" Glen mumbled

shyly (yay! he matched the style of "his" letter!). We watched – wide-eyed – as he shuffled around behind the counter, giving Mrs Patel a half-embarrassed sort of bow, before going through the doorway to the back shop and turning right into what must have been the loo.

Mrs Patel held out our change with one hand, while gently patting her husband's arm with the other. Mr Patel gave his wife a nod and a tight little smile.

Far from anyone's gaze, hidden behind the counter, I felt the pinkie finger of my right hand being squeezed gently by someone else's pinkie.

"Thanks," Nell said brightly to the Patels, as we turned to go.

Thanks for the ice lollies, and thank you for giving us something pretty *excellent* to write about in our Karma Club book. . .

The Fifth Secret

"Made you some breakfast, honey," said Mum, absently reading a Saturday magazine supplement spread on the table, needles tucked under each arm, click-clacking at top speed. An undefined, brown, fluffy knitted something was half-covering her bump.

Mum was still pretty fit and slim – bump excepted – but I noticed she had put on a tiny bit of weight here and there since she'd become pregnant. It was her upper arms where I noticed it most. The big sunflower tattoo gave it away – it was sort of stretched out slightly, as if someone had Photoshopped an image and morphed it a little wider.

"Thanks, Mum," I said, flopping down in my pyjamas in front of a pile of toast and a cactus.

I pulled the woolly green cactus off the top of my boiled egg and cracked the top of the shell with my spoon.

"Ouch! Ooow! Stop it!" squeaked a tortured voice with every tap.

"Dad!" I sighed, staring over the table.

Dad lowered his newspaper, all innocence.

"What?" he said, as if imitating an egg in pain was the *last* thing he'd think of doing.

I raised my eyebrows at him, giving him one of my

44

sternest *c'mon-grow-up!* looks, even though I thought it was pretty funny. (No wonder he had more fun working at a nursery than a kitchen wholesaler's.)

"So, how are things going with . . . um . . . your new friend?" asked Dad, ignoring my withering look and putting his paper down.

"You've forgotten her name, haven't you?" I accused him. "You never listen to a word I say!"

"And you never listen to a word *I* say, Kezzy McKenzie!" he answered good-naturedly, ruffling a hand through his already bed-messy hair (which actually stayed in pretty much the same messy style no matter what time of day it was).

"I do so!"

"Oh yeah? Well, what's the name of my new nursery nurse?"

"Er . . . Emma?" I guessed, biting my lip.

"Close . . . if you're *deaf*. It's Isabel," said Dad, with a grin and a shrug. "And where did I take my class on an outing last week?"

"The zoo?"

"The fire station. I rest my case. And the name of your new friend is?"

"It's Nell," Mum chipped in. "And she's very nice. You'll have to get her to come round here. I'd like to get to know her in a more relaxed way, like when there's no medical emergency happening. By the way—"

"Well, Isabel's off on a course on Monday," Dad butted in, making Mum roll her eyes at him. He's always doing that. He doesn't mean to be rude; it's just that he's the sort of person who needs to say something while it's in his head, or it'll just evaporate. "And if I'm not mistaken, you guys are off school for a teacher-training day, aren't you?"

We were. I'd forgotten about that. Well, this morning, at least. Yesterday, me and Nell had been full of ideas of what we could spend the day doing, and were going to meet up later and carry on the discussion.

"Mmm-hmm," I nodded at Dad, with a mouth full of egg.

"So how about you and Nell come along to the nursery and lend a hand? I've got a temp in, but you know the ropes and the kids'll love having you!"

I nodded, sure that Nell would think it was a blast (unlike Tara, who once said she'd rather pluck her nose hairs than hang out with whiny, goofy little kids like Dad did).

Once breakfast was over, I'd give Nell a ring and tell her, I thought. And I was about to have something *else* to tell her.

"*As* I was saying," Mum said pointedly to Dad.

"Sorry, Bibi!" he apologized meekly, blowing Mum a kiss.

"Well, I was in the office yesterday," Mum continued, letting go of one knitting needle long enough to pretend to catch the kiss in her hand, "and I put a couple of calls in to my social worker mates, to see if they'd heard anything from the hospital."

"About?" I prompted Mum. She means well, but she's kind of ditzy, like there's a dropped stitch in her brain from time to time.

"Well, I'd been thinking about Mrs Hooper," Mum

replied, gazing at me knowingly. Except I still didn't know what she was on about.

"Audrey?" she said, making it instantly clearer. "Sometimes, in the case of elderly patients, the hospital will get in touch with social services, to keep an eye on them when they get home. And sure enough, they had."

"And?"

From Mum's expression, it didn't seem like she was about to tell me that Audrey was doing brilliantly, and was back doing handstands and high kicks.

"Apparently, she's not great at the moment – she's too scared to go out, and she's really down."

I thought of the teen-boy-idiot who'd run Audrey over, and not even stopped to see if she was all right. He'd probably be happily cycling someplace *else* that he shouldn't this weekend, not giving a thought to old ladies whose bones would take months to heal and who might develop agoraphobia into the bargain.

It didn't seem fair.

I felt a huge wave of anger, followed by a small *ping!* of an idea.

Me and Nell needed a new good deed to do, and Audrey Hooper seemed in dire need of a good deed, if you asked me. . .

"You know what they say: when in doubt . . . panic!" Nell laughed.

I didn't get it at first. Then I realized it was just one of her dad's messed-around-with sayings. And why was she saying the, er, saying? Well, cheering up Audrey was going to be our Fifth Secret. We just had to figure out how to do it, and so far we weren't doing great with that.

"Let's just ring her buzzer and leave them at the door – and run away, of course," suggested Nell, holding the big bunch of impossibly bright yellow sunflowers behind her back.

"Look – it's a sheltered housing block. She isn't even leaving her *flat*, Mum said, so she's hardly likely to come all the way to the main entrance if we leave them here!" I told my friend as we approached the red sandstone flats where Audrey lived.

The truth was, me and Nell hadn't thought this good deed through too well; all we knew was we wanted to do something nice for Audrey, and we wanted to do it today. Not knowing what she liked (apart from biscuits), we'd decided that the safest, most reliable cheer-up present was flowers. That was till we got to the supermarket first thing that morning and found that our combined pocket money of £4 would buy her a limp, reduced bunch of £3.99 carnations, slightly brown about the petals. That would just make Audrey *more* depressed, we decided.

After that, me and Nell had mooched in the shopping centre for a while, trying to think of a Plan B, when Plan B appeared right in front of us, in the form of a tacky Pound Shop. They're always full of immensely useless but cheap things, like jumbo packs of clothes pegs (£1), three-for-the-price-of-two mega-tubs of paper clips (£1) and novelty musical notes ice cube makers (£1, but probably worth 30p).

But lo and behold . . . in a black bucket by the door was an offer that me and Nell could not refuse. Specially since it reminded me of my mum in a certain way.

"*Sunflowers: 5 for £1!!!*" the gaudy sign screamed at us.

So now we were the proud owners of twenty wildly cheerful fake flowers, and the dilemma of how to get them to Audrey. . .

"Well, I could just write a note for her, like we did on the *Big Issue* guy's hot chocolate," said Nell, scrabbling in her bag for a pen and something we could write on. "*Surely* a neighbour will come into or out of the flats at *some* point and find them. Someone's *bound* to get them to her."

I was listening, but I was also looking, letting my eyes run up and down the names by the thirty or so buzzers linked to each flat.

Ahhhh . . . there she was: "A. Hooper, Flat B (G)".

G. What was the G for? And why was it in brackets? I let my eyes skim upwards, randomly reading ". . .Flat A (1)", ". . .Flat F (2)". Call me a genius(ish), but I suddenly figured it out – "G" stood for "Ground".

"Audrey lives on the ground floor!" I announced, pointing to my proof on the metal buzzer board.

Nell and me, we looked at each other, knowing we were about to become prowlers . . . with good intentions. Well, as long as we didn't frighten any OAPs to death as we went deep undercover to discover Audrey.

"Must be out," whispered Nell, as we passed the first ground-floor flat we came to, crawling along and popping up meerkat-style to peer in the windows.

Passers-by on the nearby pavement wouldn't have been able to see us, thanks to a high hedge; we only had to worry about a bus passing, and people on the top deck getting a great view of us, looking for all the world like two teenage-girl burglars on a stake-out.

"Can't be hers . . . she's too scared to go out," I whispered back.

Two minutes and three flats later (one with a man watching wrestling, one with a lady reading a surprisingly racy-looking novel, one with a white-haired couple practising the cha-cha-cha), we hit gold.

"It's her! She's asleep!" hissed Nell, pointing into a living room with cheery rose curtains.

I crawled faster and did the meerkat thing, spotting Audrey straight away, dozing in her armchair in front of some Saturday-morning cookery show, a smug presenter babbling at some baffled contestant with a bunch of broccoli in his hand. There was a lumpy white triangle on her chest, I noticed, that baffled me till I realized it was a sling, holding her broken wrist still.

"Or maybe she's dead?" Nell said with a shrug.

I'd have hit her with the bunch of flowers, if she wasn't the one holding them. Instead, I shot her a glance that said "Oi!" . . . and at the same time rather usefully spotted something.

"Perfect!" I whispered, a smile breaking out on my face.

"That she's maybe *dead*?!" Nell frowned at me. "I was only *joking*!"

"No! That she has an empty window box!! *And* she's not dead!" I hissed back at my friend.

It was time to plant. Who knew how long Audrey was going to doze for, but when she woke up, she'd probably fancy a cup of tea. And when she went to her kitchen sink to fill the kettle, she'd see . . . well, sunshine in (fake) flower form, stuck in the earth in her window box. A vista of sunflowers that would never wilt on her, and would never need watering (maybe just a little light dusting).

Actually, we knew how much longer Audrey dozed for: one hour and twelve minutes, 'cause we were watching. Painfully.

Once our work was done and we'd snuck away, Nell had found a gap in the hedge (on the pavement side), just *leafily*-gappy enough for us to get a glimpse of Audrey's kitchen window and stay invisible – if we bent down a bit.

So one hour, twelve minutes, and lots of staring from passers-by later, both our knees (sets of knees?) had seized up (ouch), and we were just on the point of going: *that's* when we saw her.

The kitchen windows glinted in the late-morning sun like the rainbow shades in an oily puddle as Audrey pulled them open with her one good hand . . . and smiled a shy, puzzled but one-hundred-per-cent-happy smile at her instant mini-garden.

"What's that?" I asked Nell a few minutes later, as we walked contentedly towards home.

She'd just taken something out of her back pocket.

"A gold gel pen I found at home; thought it would be great for writing our good deeds down in."

I scrabbled in my bag for the gold notebook, and handed it to her.

"We should start a ratings system too," she said, flipping open the notebook at Glen and the hot chocolate. "Out of three stars, would that be a one?"

"Yep." I nodded, watching her scrawling a cute, wobbly star as we strolled. "And two stars for Mr Patel offering Glen unlimited use of his loo!"

"Right . . . two," agreed Nell, scrawling two wobbly stars on the next page.

"It has to be three out of three for Audrey," I suggested. OK, so we hadn't been able to do miracles and heal her broken bones or get the hit-and-run teen-yob arrested for reckless idiot-ness, but that smile had felt like some not-so-minor miracle.

"Three, definitely," said Nell, scribbling away. "Plus an extra one."

"What for?" I asked, immediately confused by her new system.

"For Audrey not being dead," she smirked at me.

The fourth star of the Fifth Secret wibbled *right* across the page as I thumped her arm. . .

The Sixth Secret

It was still Saturday, it was nearly one o'clock, and it was almost the end of the Rebel Knitters' regular get-together. The long table was covered in knitting patterns, yarn, empty tea cups and the remains of cake.

"*You* two look pleased with yourselves! What have you been up to?" asked Mum, glancing up at me and Nell and giving me a knowing "Hmmmm?" look.

Which I was just going to ignore, actually. I fingered the gold heart badge I had pinned on to the inside hem of my T-shirt and bit my lip. Alongside me, Nell was struggling to hide a secretive smile. But what was *particularly* funny was that she had gold glitter on her lips from sucking the end of her gel pen.

"Leave the girl alone, Bibi!" said Maura, one of the other knitting nutters – OK, members of the Rebel Knitters' Society – in an equally teasing tone.

There were about fifteen of them all contentedly click-clacking in the sunshine. I knew the names of the main regulars (Maura, who liked to knit things you wouldn't expect, like various types of fruit and even underwear; Mrs Laskaris, who knitted the most amazing lacy shawls that were like something from a different century; Sheila, who was very competitive and liked to do fearsomely complicated patterns; Elzbieta the Polish girl, who knitted very warm jumpers for very cold Polish winter visits home; and Gabrielle, who mostly spent her time dropping stitches, swearing and apologizing for swearing, according to Mum).

"You didn't move this table on your own, did you?" I asked Mum, side-stepping her question and asking one of my own.

"No – Sheila and Elzbieta came early and did it for me. Since *you* weren't *here*. . .!"

She was only teasing again, but I still felt a little prickle of guilt for standing too long peering through a hedge and forgetting what the time was – even if it *was* for a good, sunflower-y cause that Mum would be proud of. (If it wasn't a secret, I mean.)

"What *is* that brown thing, by the way?" I asked, pointing to the mystery mohair whatever that Mum was busy with.

"A tree," she said blithely.

Mum could have been teasing me again, but then she could *just* as easily have been telling the truth. She was probably about to transform the spare room into a realistic scene from *Bambi* for the baby, complete with knitted deer, rabbits and even rabbit droppings.

"Oh, Kezzy – isn't that your friend Tara?" Mum's knitting buddy Sheila blurted out, waving her hand and her latest complicated knitting pattern in the air on my behalf. Sheila always meant well – she helped out part-time in a charity shop – but I wished she hadn't bothered. "Yoo-hoo!!"

And I wished she hadn't said "Yoo-hoo!!" like that either. Turning around to see Tara (and *Robyn*, naturally), I knew what expression to expect on my ex-best mate's face: a half-hearted smile that was as genuine as an eight-pound note.

Had our friendship been as fake to her? All three years of it?

"Hi. . ." said Tara, swivelling her body from the course it was set on (i.e., steering unseen behind me, from the café out to the main park) and taking a few steps towards us.

Frowny-faced Robyn followed practically *right* in her footsteps, shadow-style – which would have been funny, if I'd felt like laughing, which I suddenly didn't. After a brilliant morning, somehow Tara and her black-rain-cloud of a best mate cast a shadow over me.

"Hi!" I said, all mock brightly. "What are you up to?"

"Just getting a juice," said Tara, half-heartedly holding up a carton of something and affecting a look of total boredom. "Then we're going into town."

"To check out stuff that Tara might want for her birthday," Robyn added.

"Of course! It's your birthday, what . . . next Sunday?" Mum chipped in.

I was glad she had – I suddenly couldn't speak. I'd had the place of pride by Tara's side when we had that dress-up disco in the church hall (three years ago); when she took all her friends bowling (two years ago); and when we went to the ice rink (last year). *This* time round, it hit me splat in the chest; I wasn't going to be by Tara's side, whatever she was doing.

I had a funny feeling that I wasn't even going to be asked at *all*, which was even weirder – not to mention harder – to think about.

"Next Saturday," Tara corrected Mum, without making any eye contact with me.

Help . . . I was instantly as close to tears as I'd felt a couple of times as a little kid, when I found out I hadn't been invited to so-and-so's princess party or whatever. How ridiculous.

But how could I switch off this feeling?

"Well, *we* better get going, 'cause we've got that thing to do, Kezzy!" said Nell, instantly reminding me of her (most excellent) existence.

One glance into her dark, purposeful eyes and the "*What* thing?" on my lips changed to a grateful, "Oh, yeah . . . so we do!"

Thank goodness for true (new) friends coming up with usefully vague white lies when I needed to keep my dignity.

"Well, see you around!" said Tara, shuffling off, wafting her juice carton at me in lieu of a proper wave.

"Bye, Tara!" Mum called out forcefully, over the top of my feeble, "Bye. . ."

Y'know, I could have *sworn* Mum clenched her jaw a little. But before I could try to read her mind any more, Nell was tugging me away.

"So where *are* we going?" I asked, following her along, my trainers scuffing the paving stones of the park café patio.

"A place of great beauty, of mystery, and of magic!" exclaimed Nell, her fingers spread wide in the air in front of us. "Otherwise known as the ladies' toilet. I'm desperate."

I laughed, and trotted behind her, realizing I needed to go too, after a hectic morning of do-gooding.

"By the way, thanks for making up that thing about us *doing* a thing. . ." I muttered self-consciously to Nell, who was now in the cubicle next to me.

I wasn't self-conscious about thanking Nell, just shy about how desperately in need of help I must have seemed to her, faced with Tara.

"No problem. But. . ."

"But what?" I encouraged Nell.

"But how come you could ever be friends with that girl? She is trying *so* hard to be 'cool' –"

Nell said the word "cool" in a hugely sarcastic voice.

"– that it's totally embarrassing to watch!"

Was *that* it? Had Tara just changed 'cause she was desperate to give off this whole new image?

It made me feel a bit better somehow. Like it wasn't so much *my* dumb fault for believing in a fake friendship for so many years as a case of Tara trying on a whole new personality, now that she was going to a whole new school, with whole new (horrible) mates like Robyn.

"Tara wasn't so much like that before. She was pretty giggly and stuff; we had fun hanging out. We watched loads of movies together – her favourites were those high-school-type things, y'know?"

I heard a vague retching sound coming from Nell's cubicle.

"It was just a laugh!" I said, feeling a tiny bit protective of the *me* that existed before last Saturday, before Nell came zooming into my life, appearing on the other side of Audrey as we tried to help her stand up.

"Go on! Tell me more interesting facts about her, so I can see her as a whole, rounded person, instead of a snidey moo!"

"She's not *that* bad!" I said, realizing I was sounding defensive.

"Yes, she is! I was watching her before your mum's friend called out to her. She was laughing at your mum and her buddies with that dumb mate of hers!"

"*Was* she?" I gasped, the soft, swirly memory of my old friendship evaporating like frosty breath over a cauldron of bile.

That was pretty funny, the idea of Tara having the cheek to take the mickey out of my mum's hobby, when hers was collecting *pigs*.

That's right: *pigs*.

She had hundreds of them in her room: china pigs, soft-toy pigs, pig socks, pig earrings, pig mobiles, piggy pictures, pig jigsaws, pig pyjamas, a knitted pig (a present from my mum on her eleventh birthday), pig slippers, pig wallpaper on her computer, pig stationery, a piggy phone and even a musical box with a tiny pig ballerina dancing to "Greensleeves". As I sat on the cold and uncomfortable loo seat in the park toilets, I wondered venomously what her super-"cool" buddy Robyn made of all *that* stuff. ("Cool" it certainly wasn't.)

"Hey! Isn't there someone called Dionna in the year above us?" I heard Nell ask out of the blue, veering away from the increasingly annoying subject of Tara.

"Yeah – Dionna Makere. Why? What about her?" I asked, getting myself together and flushing the loo.

"Someone's written on the back of my door here, something that says she's . . . well, something incredibly *rude*."

With that echoing flush I knew Nell was finished too. I slipped the lock on my cubicle door and shot through to hers, just as she opened it up for me. We both squished in, closing the door just enough so that I could read what was scrawled there.

I gasped. I didn't know Dionna very well, but she certainly wasn't . . . well, *that*.

"That's *so* not fair – or true!" I said.

"But why would someone write stuff like that about her?" asked Nell.

"'Cause their boyfriend fancied her?" I suggested, the reality dawning on me when I remembered some gossip that Shannon in my class had told me when I was hanging out with her a while back. It had got out round school that Stacey Winters' boyfriend had a sort of a *thing* for Dionna, who didn't have a clue about the thing herself.

"Bet that was Stacey Winters, or one of her friends," I said, nodding at the graffiti and feeling a whole heap of pity for Dionna. "Wish I had a tin of paint so we could make that disappear!"

"Or a gold gel pen!" Nell replied triumphantly, holding hers up.

"But . . . wouldn't that be a kind of graffiti too?" I asked her, sussing out what it was that Nell was suggesting.

"Yeah, but just like you get white lies, you get white

graffiti," she said, making up a convincing-sounding rule on the spot. Her dad, with his made-up sayings, would be proud of her.

And so we did our second good deed of the day, the fourth one that we could write about it in our notebook, which also happened to be the *Sixth* Secret of the Karma Club.

And our secret read: "*Dionna Makere is a* [this first part in black ink, followed by] *total princess!* [in gold gel pen, obliterating the rude words]".

This particular good deed might even be a secret from Dionna Makere herself – since I'd never seen her hang out in the park – but that didn't stop it feeling any less good. In fact, it felt *great*. . .

"Y'know, it's a bit like my mum," I said, leaning back against the cold, white tiles of the loo to observe our handiwork.

"What – your *mum's* had rude graffiti written about her?"

"No!" I sniggered. "I just remembered that she once told me she had her sunflower tattoo inked on over another smaller, stupider tattoo that she regretted having done."

"Which was?" Nell asked.

"I don't know!" I replied, realizing I hadn't ever asked that obvious question, just like I'd never asked Dad if he ever yearned to get back on a surfboard (big rocks permitting).

Mum's epic backpacking trips; Dad's surfing days . . . I'd heard all the stories growing up, of course, but I should ask my parents about them again sometime.

And maybe soon, before the newest member of our family appeared and their brains melted under an onslaught of night-time feeds, high-pitched yelling and never-ending nappies.

"Hold on. . ." said Nell, just as we were about to shuffle out of the cubicle.

She took the top off the gold gel pen again and wrote high up on the door: "The Karma Club rules!"

"Um, technically, that's *real* graffiti this time," I pointed out to Nell.

Nell grinned and shrugged as if it didn't matter.

But a little flutter of worry niggled in my chest: maybe it *did* matter. After all, we were supposed to do only good stuff. Wouldn't writing that message risk bringing us a dollop of *bad* karma now?

"I saw cake on your mum's table. Will we go see if there's some spare?" asked Nell, her eyes twinkling.

With my ravenous stomach suddenly somersaulting at the thought of food, I hurried away, leaving the grotty loos and the bad karma niggles behind.

How strange; despite the sunshine, the world, the park, right now everything seemed tinged light grey. . .

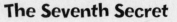

The Seventh Secret

"Nell, Neil; Neil, Nell!" Mum giggled, introducing my friend to my dad and vice versa.

She had a red knitted band tied around her pinned-up hair today, which was fixed at one side in a cutely floppy bow. She'd knocked it up in about twenty minutes flat last night while we were all watching some Saturday night film.

"Neil McKenzie, at your service," said Dad, grabbing Nell's hand and bowing down low to her.

Now it was Nell's turn to giggle.

We were doing the introductions all squished in the hall, as Nell had rung my doorbell just as Mum and Dad were on their way out to IKEA to buy baby-friendly stuff for the impending arrival of my sister. (Seven weeks and counting.)

"We'll be a couple of hours, I guess," Mum told me, grabbing her (knitted) daisy-patterned bag from a coat hook by the door. "So if you girls fancy some lunch or snacks or anything, help yourselves."

"OK, Mum," I said, giving her a peck on the cheek and pulling a face at my dad. He pulled one right back.

After a jumble of byes, I shut the door, and proceeded to give Nell the guided tour – though she'd already started without me.

"Wow!" she gasped at the knitted *Mona Lisa* on the wall, at the knitted tarantula and goldfish cushions on the sofas, at the knitted personalized placemats on the table.

"Yep," I said to her wow.

"Who knits *curtains*?!" she gasped, holding out Mum's stripy, '60s Pop Art-inspired flowing sheets of wool.

"My mum, obviously," I replied, hands shoved in my jeans' pockets. "She's done them in every room except mine. I just wanted a roller blind at my window, and she hasn't figured out how to knit one of *those* yet. . ."

We got up to my room eventually, once Nell had gasped and exclaimed her way around the place (she particularly loved the knitted trailing ivy in the bathroom). Now we were hunkered down on the window seat that Dad had fixed up for me a couple of months ago, with the five fluffy mini-cushions Mum had made to go with it (they spelt out KEZZY if you laid them in the right order). Nell was currently sitting cross-legged with a fuchsia pink "Z" in her lap and the gold notebook and pen lying in the space between us.

"Hold on a second. . ." I grunted, stretching up on to my knees and pulling the stiff window shut. It wasn't at all chilly – it just helped drown out the yap-yap-yapping of the Ugly Barky Dog further up the street.

"What's this?" asked Nell, fingering a raised Lurex thread doodle sewn in the bottom right-hand corner of the "Z" cushion.

"My mum's signature – Bibi Lee. She's just started doing it on her stuff," I explained, settling back down and helping myself to another biscuit from the packet

I'd taken up with us. (Well, we seemed to need to fortify ourselves with food when we were thinking about our good-deeds-to-be. Yes, I know – *any* excuse. . .)

"Bibi Lee! What a great name. Is Bibi your mum's actual name, or short for something?"

"Short for Belinda – but no one calls her that except for my grandparents and a couple of her old mates from school."

Actually, Belinda became Bibi back during her time waitressing in Cornwall: the boss's little kid couldn't get her tiny tongue around Mum's name – the closest she got was "Bee-Bee!" Dad had never known Mum as anything else and *still* sometimes wondered who Granny and Grandad were talking about when we went for a visit to theirs.

"But wait – your mum's last name's Lee, but *yours* isn't. Aren't your parents married?"

"Nope." I shook my head. "They don't see the point. Mum especially – she always says that the important thing is to remember to love each other, not to worry about proving it with a bit of paper."

It was my standard line if the subject cropped up. I mean, most people didn't really care one way or the other, but occasionally you got raised eyebrows, mostly from parents or grannies or whatever. Tara's mum seemed a bit tight-lipped about it when the subject came up once, I remember. ("So . . . your mum and dad aren't *married*?" she'd said, in the same tone of voice she might have said, "So . . . your mum and dad, they don't wear *pants*?!")

But hey, even though we'd known each other for just

a week, I got the feeling that Nell wasn't going to be like Mrs Dixon and make a big deal of it.

"Yeah, same with *my* mum and dad," she surprised me by saying, now helping herself to a biscuit too.

I hadn't expected that.

"Yeah?" I said, thinking that big-shot managers like her dad tended to live pretty predictable lives, didn't they? Nice house, nice car, nice wife, nice kid(s). I mean, apart from her dad having that brief rock 'n' roll moment in his youth, Nell had made both her parents sound pretty straight and normal. Nice, but normal. Whereas mine were . . . well, nice, but just slightly to the *left* of normal.

"Mmm," mumbled Nell, through a mouthful of crumbs. "They say they don't see the point either. But I sometimes think Mum quite fancies the idea. . . She always goes a bit twinkly-eyed when there're weddings on the telly. I quite fancy it myself, if they did it somewhere like on a beach in Antigua or the Maldives!"

"Don't think mine will *ever* get round to it," I shrugged, a sudden image popping into my head of Mum carrying a bouquet of knitted roses.

"So what are they going to call the baby?" asked Nell, brushing a stray brown curl from her mouth.

"They're both big on old-fashioned names like Dulcie and Cora—"

"And Kezzy?"

"*Keziah*," I said with a nod, giving my full name. "But they're just going to wait and see what suits the baby when she's born."

"Screaming Blob, then!" Nell joked.

I laughed, but let my eyes wander to the scene outside. For the last couple of minutes that we'd been talking, I'd watched the Harassed Single Mum come out of the house across the road with her brood of small people (they bounced about so much it was hard to count them, but I was pretty sure there were four of them, who all looked like they were under *five*).

She'd tried to hustle them all – *screaming* – past the Ugly Barky Dog's gate (the faint sound of yelping sped up). She then packed them – plus buggy and empty shopping bags – into her very small, very dirty car, parked in the cul-de-sac opposite. I guess when you've got so many kids to take care of on your own, having a car that's got three years' worth of dirt and grime on it is pretty understandable.

"Hey, I forgot to ask you something yesterday," I said distractedly to Nell. "Dad was wondering if we wanted to come and help him at his nursery tomorrow?"

"Sure! That'd be fun! Do we get to tie up the naughty kids?" Nell joked again.

Through the closed window, I could now hear the Harassed Single Mum's many, *many* attempts to start the car engine. It wouldn't budge.

Uh-oh . . . she was coming back *out* of the car, and looked just about ready to bang her head off the roof. One by one, she unbuckled the kids and yanked them out again, along with the buggy and the empty shopping bags. Guess they were all off *walking* to the supermarket. *That* was going to be a fun trip, with four kids acting like whining puppies.

With that brood and bad luck like broken-down, dirty cars to contend with, no *wonder* Harassed Single Mum looked so harassed all the time. . .

"I've got it! I know the next one!" I suddenly announced, slapping my hand on the Karma Club notebook. . .

The Seventh Secret of the Karma Club had been wet and tiring to do.

But now me and Nell were back at the window seat, sitting bare-legged, eating strawberries and yoghurt and waiting for our jeans to finish spinning around in the tumble dryer.

"Your hair looks funny!" I said, nodding at her half-flat, half-curly concoction.

"I think you'd call it *hood*hair," she said with a grin. "Anyway, you've still got a streak of dirt down the side of your face."

"Have I?" I asked. I'd get up and wash that off in a minute. We didn't need Mum or Dad to come back and catch us out with awkward questions about what we'd been up to. Nope, they'd bumble back in with their IKEA bags and boxes, and find us innocently sitting in our newly dried jeans, with shiny clean faces. The cagoules we'd hidden ourselves under (with hoods up, even in the bright sunshine, for fear of neighbours recognizing us and spoiling the secret) were back in the cupboard under the stairs, as was the yellow bucket and the sponge Dad used to clean our car. Two pairs of rubber gloves – one yellow, one pink – were folded up in the old basin under the sink, where we'd found them.

And out in the cul-de-sac was one very sparkly, clean, shiny car. OK, it might still be small, old and broken-down, but hey – it wasn't like we two members of the Karma Club were mechanics, was it?

"Here she comes!" I said excitedly, pausing with a spoonful of strawberries and yoghurt halfway to my mouth.

Nell craned her neck round to see – and there was the Harassed Single Mum trudging along past the Ugly Barky Dog, pushing a buggy weighed down with heavy shopping bags, with a trail of miserable, whiny kids dragging along beside her. Her shoulders were sagging, her mouth was the exact opposite of smiling and she was doing a fantastic impression of someone being sucked slowly into a sludgy vat of gloom.

And then she saw it. The car. She had been crossing the top of the cul-de-sac and hadn't noticed for a second. Then she did a double-take, standing completely still, before letting go of the buggy and slowly walking around the car that she only half-recognized as hers.

She stopped, put her hands on her hips, and stared.

"What's she doing now?" I wondered, as the woman put her hands over her eyes.

"Playing peek-a-boo?" Nell suggested uselessly, as three of the four kids gaggled up around her.

"No – she's *crying*!!" I said, recognizing the telltale, up-and-down shake of her shoulders.

"Wow! That's a *good* thing, right?" Nell muttered dubiously.

Actually, I wasn't entirely sure whether to be proud or

freaked out that our kind deed had made the Harassed Single Mum *cry*.

"*Whaaaaaaaaaah!*"

It was a loud, indignant yell from the temporarily forgotten little kid strapped in the buggy.

It wasn't yelling 'cause it had been forgotten, but because its buggy had just tipped right back thanks to the weight of all the shopping bags.

"Oops! Our good deed nearly broke the baby!" Nell winced.

As the Harassed Single Mum and the marginally older kids raced to save the little one, I saw something else to make us panic.

Mum and Dad's car, cruising down the street.

"Jeans! *Now!*" I burst out, leaping off the window seat in a flurry of biscuit crumbs. . .

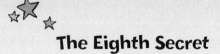

The Eighth Secret

We were in a room jam-packed full of puppies.

Most of them were lolloping about, a couple were play-fighting, a couple more were howling, one was chasing its tail, another was eating something off the floor, while another was asleep in the corner. Oh, and unknown to anyone at this point, another one had had a little accident over by the building blocks. . .

OK, so they weren't *technically* puppies, but pretty much as good as. The sixteen three-year-olds in Dad's nursery class this morning were as dopey and cute as any dog I'd seen (well, except for the Ugly Barky Dog in our street, who was probably *never* cute, even when he was a pup).

"Right, children!" Dad yelled out with a brash shake of his tambourine. "Snack and story time! Everyone on the carpet, please!"

Quite a few of the puppies/kids did as they were told and stopped lolloping about, instead flopping next to their buddies on the cartoony flowered carpet.

In the half-hour since we'd been here, me and Nell had helped make:

- pretty, glittery pictures
- sandcastles

- a fire engine out of toilet roll tubes
- play-dough cookies
- a mess (well, it's tough with all that glitter and glue and sand etc).

But from the times I'd helped Dad out before, I knew that *this* was the point when he needed his staff (both professional *and* useless-but-willing) to act like sheepdogs and herd stragglers over to the carpet.

Actually, the one professional member of staff (the temp nursery nurse that Dad had hired in for the day) had gone to chop up fruit for the children, which left the useless-but-willing members of staff (me and Nell) to do the rounding up.

"You get the ones on *that* side of the room," I ordered Nell, pointing at one of the two kids who were crying, as well as the one eating small bits of play dough off the floor, *and* the one who was sleeping on the cushions over in the book corner. Dad was already separating the two who were thumping each other with plastic dinosaurs, which left *me* to scoop up the other howler, plus the little girl running happily in circles . . . and the boy I'd just spotted hiding behind the cupboard that the building blocks got tidied away in at the end of each session.

"Yes, sir!" said Nell, giving me a quick salute and cheerfully going off to do her duty.

Keeping an eye on the head of hair I saw peeking out from behind the building blocks cupboard, I gently led the howler to the carpet and helped her blow her nose. Then it was back to the girl running in circles, who was *less* keen to be led anywhere, but *did* come after she'd kicked me in the shins a couple of times.

Lastly, it was the turn of the kid hiding (not very well) behind the cupboard.

"Hi there! Are you going to come and listen to a lovely story? Mr McKenzie's got a really nice one today!" I said, holding out my hand to the small person with the downturned head and thumb wedged in his mouth.

I hadn't a clue what story Dad was going to be reading out, but I suspected I'd be safe in saying it was nice, because picture books tend to be full of cute mice and funny space rockets and stuff and not really chainsaw massacres or anything scary like that.

The little kid ignored me and kept his head down, as if that would help make him invisible.

"Aren't you coming?" I asked gently, kneeling down on the floor beside him. Which was a bit of a mistake, to be honest.

"Yew!" I muttered, feeling the knee of my jeans go instantly soggy.

"Joe – aren't you coming to join us?" I heard Dad call out, spotting I was stuck with the last straggler.

"He won't come! Joe did a wee-wee on the floor again!" a little boy piped up from his cross-legged spot on the floor, to a ripple of giggles and sniggers.

Urgh . . . I'd just discovered this shy kid Joe's little "accident" with my *knee*. Fantastic.

"Um, Nell," said Dad, getting to his feet and holding an oversized book out to my friend, "can you sit up here on the chair and read the story – in a big, bright, loud voice, please – while I get Joe sorted out?"

"I'll get the mop," I offered, as Dad came over our way.

"Great, but first, could you do me a favour and look out a spare pair of pants and trousers from the box in the office? Just bring them to us in the toilets in a second," said Dad, gently taking hold of the little boy's hand (the boy *still* hadn't raised his head and his thumb was still wedged firmly in his mouth).

"Sure," I nodded, feeling so bad for the little boy (the giggles started up again as Dad led him off to the loos) that I almost forgot my yucky damp patch.

"Thanks, Kezzy," said Dad, as I passed the clean, dry clothes over the top of the cubicle door a couple of minutes later. "Joe is a such a good lad, aren't you, Joe?"

From the other side of the sky blue cubicle door I heard, well, *nothing* in answer to that question.

"Just step in there . . . *and* the other one . . . that's it. You see, Kezzy, there's just one little problem we've got to sort out," Dad carried on, talking first to Joe and then to me. "Joe's a little bit shy – aren't you, Joe? – and often finds it hard to ask to go to the loo when the need arises!"

The sound of a zip.

"There – you're all done, Joe! Good as new!"

Poor kid. You're shy, so you're too scared to ask to go to the toilet, so you have an accident, so the kids laugh at you, which makes you even *more* shy than ever.

Y'know, I hadn't even made eye contact with this kid yet, but I knew that somehow, I'd love the Eighth Secret of the Karma Club to have something to do with *him*. But what could that be, exactly?

I'd have to have a hard think, just as soon as I'd mopped up the wee and held my knee under the hot-air dryer for a bit. . .

His hair was brown. We could make out that he had a nose. And a *thumb*, of course, since it was in his mouth. But that was as close a description as we had of the little dude Joe, since we'd *still* never got a full-on look at his face yet.

Of course, there was the greyish smoky haze of misery hanging around him, but maybe only *I* could see that.

"Dad said he started here a couple of months ago, and he's mostly held his head down like that for the whole time," I told Nell. "He is one *seriously* shy kid."

We were on playground duty while Dad and his assistant set up more activities inside. Being on playground duty seemed to consist of leaning against the wall and doing a lot of watching: watching the little kids lollop around in the sunshine, slip down the slides, run around with dolls in toy buggies, or fight over whose turn it was for the trikes.

Unless you were a kid called Joe, that is. If you were a kid called Joe, then you were sitting alone on a bench with your head down and your fists clenched in your lap.

No one, it seemed, wanted to play with someone who'd had an "accident".

"Hold on, I've got sweets in my bag. . ." said Nell, disappearing back inside the nursery.

Great. I'd hoped we could think up a secret good deed to help out Joe, and all Nell could think about was *sweets*.

I managed to break up a trike fight, help dress a baby doll and coo over a ladybird that a girl called Madeleine had found before Nell reappeared. Bizarrely, she had something – possibly a *couple* of somethings – up the inside of her T-shirt. She gazed around the playground for a second, and then seemed to spot whatever it was she was looking for.

"Kezzy – meet me over by the vegetable patch in two minutes. Bring Joe over, and tell him you need him to help find toys."

"What toys?" I asked, trying to figure out what she had planned.

"I don't know . . . *lost* toys!" she said hurriedly, before scooting over towards the vegetable patch holding her T-shirt.

Whatever she was doing, it had to stay secret – that much I knew. So for the next little while, I quickly encouraged a couple of kids to have a trike race and whooped and hollered encouragement loud enough to get most kids' attention fixed on the mini Tour de France that was happening.

All except Joe.

"Joe, I need you to come and help me look for . . . um . . . some lost toys," I said vaguely, checking to see that Nell was finished doing whatever it was that she'd been doing. Yep – she was close to the vegetable patch, but pretending to brush sand off an old, worn teddy.

Joe slowly and falteringly stood up and took my hand, reluctantly following where I led.

"Now, Mr McKenzie said that the, er, lost toys could

be anywhere," I muttered brightly. "So why don't we check the vegetable patch to see if any have been chucked in there?"

Yes! Well done to Kezzy. . .

I saw what Nell had done before Joe did, being more than twice his size.

"Hey . . . what's this?" I gasped in my best what's-Santa-left-you? type voice. I dropped his floppy hand and parted the long, green tangles of courgette leaves.

"Oh!"

It was only a tiny sound from the kid Joe, but it was a *good* sound.

And with the sound, his head rose up, and a smile broke out on his pale face. The grey, smoky haze of misery swirled off into the sky, to be replaced with the tiniest pink roses in his cheeks.

"What does it say?" I asked, pretending I couldn't read the words spelt out in multicoloured Smarties, above the Smarties smiley face on the paper plate.

"I don't know!" he said, turning to face me, with a hopeful expression. "Is it my name?"

"It says 'Hi Joe!'," said Nell, appearing by our sides. "Wow – how cool is that?! Hey, kids! Come and see what Joe's just found!"

He had a nice face, Joe. And with that big, hopeful smile on it he suddenly went from being the seriously shy kid to someone that looked almost familiar.

"Oooh!", "What-is-it? What-is-it?", "Joe's name!", "And a funny face!", "Made of sweets!", "Cool!" cooed all the kids, bumbling and scurrying over for a peek.

Joe beamed under all the attention, positively

beamed. Which is exactly what Nell had planned to happen, I guess.

"Well, I don't know how this got here," said my friend, using the teacherly voice she'd come out with so impressively when she'd been reading the story at snack time earlier, "but this face and these sweets definitely are meant to be for you, Joe. So do you think you'd like to share them out?"

As Nell reached over to gently lift the paper plate, Joe's smile slipped away a little as his eyes widened and his mouth slipped into another "Oh!" of surprise. It was then that I realized why he'd looked so familiar – he was the little kid from the play park. The one who'd nearly been run over instead of Audrey the old lady. The boy who'd run off crying when I'd tried to offer him a crisp, and backed off from Nell when she'd offered to stop the roundabout to let him get on.

As the coincidence dawned on me, my tummy did a backflip, which tied in nicely with the somersault in my chest, caused by the fact that what Nell had just suggested was pretty high up on the list of no-nos (No Hitting, No Biting, No Pushing, No Eating Sweets) at Dad's nursery.

"They're not really allowed to have those!" I said, vividly remembering the "No Eating Sweets" rule a second too late, as Nell gave the plate to Joe, and Joe was suddenly surrounded by grateful new buddies.

"Hey, so we're breaking *one* little rule – but it's in a good cause!" Nell replied with a small, so-what? shrug.

A niggle narled away inside me again, same as it had done on Saturday (grey cloud, grey cloud), when Nell hadn't just altered the rude graffiti about Dionna Makere

77

but had added some of her own too. We shouldn't really be breaking any rules – no matter how teeny-weeny – not when it came to our good deeds. I didn't want any bad karma coming our way . . .

Or maybe I was just fretting over nothing?

It sure felt like that when Dad saw the change in Joe, when we shooed all the kids back into class at the end of the break. ("What happened out there?" Dad asked, marvelling at the kids hanging around Joe and asking him to join in their games. We just shrugged.)

And I felt that my worries were pretty petty at the end of the morning session, when a shyly smiling Joe ran into the arms of his pleasantly stunned mum.

And that led to a moment of me being stunned too.

No . . . it couldn't be, could it?!

"Dad!" I said, nudging up beside him as he chatted and nodded at the parents and carers coming to pick up.

"Uh-huh?" murmured Dad, continuing with his nodding and smiling and helping on with jackets. "You're looking a bit red around your neck – are you OK?"

Ah, the red splatches . . . my allergy to coincidences was striking again.

Big time.

"Yeah, yeah. Anyway, that kid Joe's mum – she lives near us!" I said in total surprise, staring at the Harassed Single Mum as she beamed happily into the face of her kid. How could I *not* have put two and two (or two and two and even *more*) together? Maybe because Joe was just part of the hectic bundle of kids when I spotted him out with his bundlesome family in the road?

"I know! I *told* you her little boy had started at nursery with us!"

"Did you? When?" I asked, bewildered and racking my brains.

"A couple of months ago – what was I saying the other day about you never listening to a word I s—"

I stopped listening again and walked over to tell Nell all.

"Where's the notebook?" I asked her. "'Cause today's good deed needs *serious* gold stars!"

"Yeah. How many out of three, d'you reckon?" she asked, as a kid who'd been sleeping in the book corner started climbing up her like she was a girl-shaped mountain.

I glanced over at the Harassed Single Mum, who was hugging her giggling little boy, and realized it looked like we'd made her cry again.

"Five!" I told her. "At *least*. . .!"

The Ninth Secret

A small, scrawled note slithered across the desk towards me.

"*I don't believe you,*" it said.

I shot a look at Miss Lennard, but she was absently staring out of the window, as if she wished she were on a desert island, or the moon, or on her hands and knees painting double-yellow lines on the road outside with her toothbrush; *anywhere*, basically, other than this particular classroom on this particular Tuesday morning with us.

Underneath Nell's scrawl, I did one of my own.

"*Don't believe what?*"

"*That Miss Lennard is usually OK. She's a miserable old moo. And her lessons are booooooorrrrrrrinnnnggggggggg. . .*"

There wasn't room on the scrap of paper to explain that usually, Miss Lennard was one of the best teachers in school, who never droned on and on and made you wish you were on a desert island or the moon or on your hands and knees painting double-yellow lines on the road outside with your toothbrush or *anywhere* except in that lesson at that precise time. She didn't drown you in homework (like some teachers), and she organized field trips and talks and films every term (which plenty of teachers couldn't be bothered doing). I knew that normally she'd be perched on the front of her desk, hands waving as she talked, so animated about history that she got you all animated too.

"She never usually sits all slouched down behind her desk like that," I told Nell, three hours and fifteen minutes later, as we spent our lunch time in the pleasant but unexpected pursuit of stalking Miss Lennard.

I know stalking's bad, but blame the curry. There was a new cook at school who'd changed the recipe from a fab coconutty chicken thing to an indiscriminately meaty hot sludge that burned the back of your throat off. Since we were a) quite attached to our throats, and b) our school was cool about us leaving at lunch time (unlike some other local schools), me and Nell decided to give lunch a miss and go get a takeaway sandwich or something from the Parade Café next door to Mr Patel's.

I'd never thought about it before, but teachers must eat the same food as us at lunch time, and it looked like Miss Lennard didn't much fancy having the back of her mouth burned off either. We'd spotted her ambling along in front of us, on her way somewhere past the procession of little shops, and decided to amble along quite close behind her, just to see where she went, and if being out of school cheered her up any.

(Actually, *I'd* cheered up, now I realized we could legitimately call it coincidental *ambling* rather than *stalking*. . .)

"I quite like the way she dresses," muttered Nell, eyeing up Miss Lennard's baggy olive-coloured linen trousers, short, puff-sleeved cream cotton shirt, flat leather sandals and slouchy canvas shoulder bag.

"She always has cool jewellery too," I told Nell,

thinking of the chunky amber beads Miss Lennard was wearing today, and the various other necklaces and bracelets I always checked out during lessons.

"Hey . . . she's diverting," said Nell, as we watched Miss Lennard smile at Glen the *Big Issue* bloke and go past him into Mr Patel's shop. "What do you suppose she's getting? A bunch of red pens to mark our homework with?"

"Don't know – but let's pretend to be looking in here when she comes out," I suggested, pointing to the window of the chemist shop just before Mr Patel's.

Glen – who was only a couple of metres away – gave me a nod and a smile of recognition. I blushed crimson and did a stupid jerky nod in response that probably looked like I had a nervous twitch. God . . . I bet he thought I had a little crush on him or something, instead of just feeling self-conscious at the fact that his name was written down twice in the gold notebook that my left hand was clutching right now.

"Wow! Look at that!" I said, pointing to something in the chemist's window.

"What? The talc? Or the two-for-one offer on gum disease mouthwash?" Nell laughed.

"It's just our cover, for when Miss Lennard comes back out!" I whispered at her.

Actually, I wasn't staring at the talc or the gum disease mouthwash. I was idly gazing at the glass shelf of gifts that the chemist-shop owner also kept in the window. I always thought it was weird when chemists did that; had gifts, I mean. It's just, do people *really* think about picking up a birthday present when they're in buying verruca cures and nappy rash cream?

Still . . . in amongst the travel clocks, plastic flower arrangements and jewellery boxes was something I *might* have bought someone, once upon a time. It was a tiny pink pottery pig, with a pattern of yellow buttercups all over it.

Tara would love that. . . I thought, finding myself remembering that it was only a few days till her birthday. Strangely enough (not), I still hadn't had an invite to . . . well, whatever she was doing for it.

"She's out. Miss Lennard's out!" Nell hissed, nudging me.

Luckily, Nell was able to surreptitiously watch our teacher while pretending to talk to me about something in the shop window.

"Where's she going? Should we follow?" I hissed back.

"Wait . . . she's got a newspaper, but she's stopped to buy a *Big Issue* from that Glen guy," Nell murmured, keeping her lips pretty much still as she spoke, like a ventriloquist. It was quite impressive. "Oh, OK . . . now she's walking away, so we can go after – no, stop! She's gone into the Parade Café!"

Uh-oh, we were being watched. Glen was sort of casually smiling at us, I guess wondering what we were up to. Which made *me* question what we were up to.

"This is silly!" I announced in my more normal voice. "Why don't we just go in too? We were going to go in there for a sandwich anyway, and I'm starving!"

Nell gazed at me with a slight hint of disappointment.

Who knows what we thought we might find out about Miss Lennard (and her current gloom) by stalking – I mean, coincidentally ambling behind her this lunch time, but I suppose it had been marginally more exciting than our usual school dinners and loitering in the playground till the afternoon bell went.

"Yeah, whatever," she said with a shrug, starting to walk in the direction of the café.

I deliberately didn't look Glen's way as we passed him, in case he was still labouring under the false impression that I might have a pink-cheeked crush on him. But out of the corner of my eye, I couldn't help notice that he didn't seem quite as permanently cold and pale ice-blue as he used to. In fact, he seemed slightly golden, with a few weeks' tan on his face. I'd have been pleased to see that, if I hadn't gone and chosen that second to trip on a paving stone right in front of him.

"Got you," giggled Nell, catching my arm before I did an ungainly splat.

I dropped the notebook, though . . . I had to do a lightning-speed scoop to retrieve it from the pavement before Glen saw his name – and Mr Patel's – written on the page that it had fallen open at. . .

My heart was still pounding five seconds later, when we walked into the café. And it began to pound even *faster* as we found ourselves standing *right* behind Miss Lennard in the queue for the takeaway counter.

Of course, the most natural and adult thing to do would have been to say an immediate "Hello!" to her, to avoid any awkwardness.

Instead, me and Nell found ourselves with sneaky

sniggers lurking in our chests when we saw what section of the newspaper she was standing reading. . .

It kind of made sense. It would explain the weird mood she'd been in, I realized, thinking of Miss Lennard this morning, her left hand propping up her fed-up face as she gazed at the clouds fluffing past the school building. Her left hand. . . I always *did* check out her jewellery, didn't I? And a ring . . . or *lack* of it, on the left hand, meant. . .

OK, so now it really *properly* made sense.

So *that* was Miss Lennard's secret.

Nell and I swapped wide-eyed gazes and telepathically knew we had to back away silently and unseen out of the café *fast*, so we could . . .

a) plan the Ninth Secret of the Karma Club, and
b) not get caught giggling over poor Miss
    Lennard's semi-tragic secret. . .

We were in a James Bond movie. We were casing the casino, nervously waiting for the coast to be clear, so we could plant the bomb and rid the world of the Bad Guys.

Nah. . .

I mean, *yes*, it was a nerve-racking and tense situation, but it wasn't so much a James Bond movie as the corridor outside the school staffroom. And we weren't casing a casino but eyeing up the door to the staffroom, and more importantly, the teachers' pigeonholes that were *just* inside the staffroom door, stuffed with random bits of post and visible every time a teacher went in and out.

And it wasn't so much a *bomb* we wanted to plant as a piece of fruit.

"Hello, girls!" said Mr Greene, one of the youngish art department teachers, as he strode by us and into the staffroom.

"Hello!" we both squeaked, suddenly pretending we were busy looking at a message on my phone and not lurking with intent at all. No way.

Was this it? Our chance? Nope. . . Mrs Mehta from the geography department was just on her way out. She hovered for a second – a second where the staffroom door slowly, tantalizingly swung closed – and rifled around in her folder of papers.

Me and Nell, we carried on pretending to check out my phone message, till Mrs Mehta set off and we could relax (and wait) again.

"So do you think *she* chucked her fiancé, or the other way round?" asked Nell, now polishing the red shiny apple with the bottom of her black and yellow striped tie.

"The other way round, *definitely*!" I whispered, though currently there wasn't anyone around but us. It was sunny outside, and the occasional teacher aside, no one particularly fancied mooching about in the dull corridors on such a nice day. "If *she'd* chucked *him*, Miss Lennard would feel guilty, but relieved and happy. If *he* chucked *her*, then she'd be miserable and spend her time staring out windows."

That was *my* theory, at least, which made sense, considering that twenty minutes ago, we'd spotted Miss Lennard in the café so earnestly scouring the "Lonely

Hearts" dating section of the local paper, *and*, more importantly, circling a couple of possibilities with her red pen.

Her engagement ring had been really pretty, I suddenly remembered. Kind of ornate, kind of antique-looking. Though now there was only a white, bare line where she'd once worn it.

"Or maybe he did something *so* bad she *had* to chuck him?" Nell suggested, tossing the apple in the air and catching it again, which made the brown label we'd tied to the stalk flutter in the air. "Hey – I just thought of something that could make this message even *better*!"

Just after we'd rushed out of the café, we'd nipped in and bought the label from Mrs Patel (who'd tried to read upside down what Nell was writing on it in her gold pen as I paid).

"What?" I asked now, as Nell caught the apple again in one hand and rifled around for something in her pocket with the other.

"Well, I was thinking: why does the message have to be anonymous?"

"Because our good deeds are *always* meant to be a secret?" I suggested, wondering what Nell was getting at.

"Yeah, but just for fun, why don't we put someone's name on it? Someone cute . . . like that Mr Greene?"

Nell looked really excited by this dumb idea. She even had her gold pen out, ready to add some more lettering (and mischief) to the label.

"Because he *didn't write the message*!" I pointed out urgently, imagining a horribly embarrassing scenario where Miss Lennard got the wrong idea entirely about the cute-ish art teacher.

"Yeah, but Glen didn't write that letter to Mr Patel either, and *that* worked out all right!" Nell insisted.

"But that was different!" I replied, not explaining myself very well, simply because I was feeling slightly panicked. That little grey-cloud bad-karma niggle was back and making itself felt inside my chest, and apart from that, time was running out. The afternoon bell was about to go, and me and Nell had set ourselves a mission that might be impossible to do. . .

Or maybe not.

Two teachers were coming out of the staffroom chatting – and there was Miss Lennard's pigeonhole, right by the door and *right* at waist-level, as if karma (the good kind, not the bad) was lending us a hand.

"*Now!*" Nell whispered insistently, getting ready to do her part. (Thankfully, without having time to add Mr Greene's name to the label.)

"OH, NO!" I gasped theatrically, as the contents of my pencil case "accidentally" spilled all over the corridor floor.

"Oh, dear!", "Oops-a-daisy!!" cried the two teachers, who seemed sympathetic but weren't in a hurry to help me scramble my things together.

But that didn't matter – as long as they were distracted enough not to notice Nell silently slipping behind them and catching the door *just* before it snibbed shut, and slipping the apple unseen into Miss Lennard's pigeonhole.

And not a second too soon.

Brinnnggggggg!!!

The afternoon bell exploded in a flurry of footsteps and chairs squeaking. Sheer adrenalin got us out of there as quickly as possible, after scooping up as many of my pens as I could.

Actually, I lost my favourite one – the one with the dumb, fluffy pink feathers on the end – but it was worth it. Worth it to see Miss Lennard two minutes later, striding towards her classroom, with a puzzled little smile on her lips and an apple-shaped bump in her beige canvas bag.

Hope she liked the message.

And hope she didn't ever match up the words "*By the way, you're lovely!!*" to the handwriting in Nell's project on The Industrial Revolution. . .

The Tenth Secret

The Tenth Secret of the Karma Club: it happened on Friday, which just *happened* to be the first rainy day in ages. The usual summer-blue skies we'd got used to faded, replaced with pavement-dull clouds and the relentless drip-drip-drip of a soggy downpour.

It was also the day me and Nell had our first-ever argument, and all because I'd kept the Tenth Secret kind of . . . well, kind of *secret* from Nell. . .

"You must be Kezzy. Been swimming?" joked the man who opened the door to me, as I dripped on his doorstep. I noticed (through the rain coursing down my face) that he had the same softly curly dark hair as Nell, only cut a lot shorter. He didn't dress much like her, though – he was wearing a suit and open-necked shirt. He was also twirling a set of car keys around one of his fingers; he must have just got home from work.

A thundering of steps on the stairs behind him meant Nell was hurrying down to meet me, for my first visit to her house. She appeared directly in front of me, after ducking under the arm that was holding the door open.

"Ignore him, he thinks he's funny," she told me, raising her eyebrows at her dad. I noticed her rubbing her fingers on the sleeve of her T-shirt, to let me know that's where her Karma Club badge was pinned. I shoved my hands in the meet-in-the-middle pocket of my cotton hoodie, to show her my gold heart badge was pinned *there*.

"Well, I have my moments," said Nell's dad with a shrug, oblivious to our secret "hello", and ruffling his hand through the top of Nell's hair so that it turned into a messy pile of tangles over her face.

"Oi!" protested Nell, shoving it back into place with her hand. "This is my dad, Kezzy, if you hadn't guessed."

"John," said her dad, closing the door and holding his hand out to take my uselessly soaked jacket from me. "Nell – get a towel for your friend's hair."

"Er, thanks. . ." I muttered, trailing off, not quite able to bring myself to use his first name. It's just too weird to call your friends' parents by their first names, unless you've known them since you were little or something. (By the way, Tara called my mum and dad Bibi and Neil, but I never called hers anything but Mr and Mrs Dixon. Calling them Diane and Ted would have seemed as rude as rifling through their knicker drawers.)

"You know, when my firm asked me to relocate," Nell's dad carried on conversationally, while Nell went off in search of a towel, "I had the choice of here or Madrid. And looking at the weather today, I think maybe I made a mistake. . ."

It was another sort of jokey remark, which made me feel kind of at home. Day-to-day life in our house was pretty much full of jokey remarks. Only this morning, Dad had called Mum "Anna". When she asked why, he said her shape reminded him of a wildlife programme he'd seen where an anaconda had just swallowed a small warthog.

"Um, so what is it you do?" I asked shyly, joining in the conversation with the first thing I could think of.

Actually, at the same time, it suddenly dawned on me that Nell's dad's full name was John Smith. The most boring and common two names in the English language. How unimaginative were Nell's grandparents?

"Telecommunications," Nell's dad replied.

He must have seen my eyes glaze over.

"I *know*," he laughed. "Sounds both complicated and yet dull, doesn't it? It's actually pretty interesting when you get into it, but I can't say it was the career I dreamed of when I was a teenager!"

"What *did* you want to be?" I asked, pushing my dripping fringe off my face. Ah, here came Nell with a towel.

"You wanted to be stuntman, didn't you?" Nell teased him.

"Yep, for a while, when I was about your age!" he agreed, slipping his jacket off. "Till I fell off my bike and realized I didn't like pain much."

"And then you wanted to be a helicopter pilot," said Nell.

"Till I took a trip in one and felt like I'd never stop being sick."

"*And* you wanted to be a famous musician!" Nell chipped in.

"Unfortunately, I was never destined to be that, thanks to a lack of playing ability and a very un-rock 'n' roll name," John Smith sighed in mock sadness. "No, all I was *really* good at was backpacking. I travelled for a year after university, and loved it. But sadly, no one pays you a wage to see different countries and have an amazing time!"

"My mum did a lot of travelling around when she was younger too!" I said excitedly as I rubbed my hair dry.

"Really? Where did your mum—"

"Oh, hello!" said a woman, barging through the front door with a bunch of bags stuffed with groceries. "Sorry I'm late!"

"Better late than disappearing in the Bermuda Triangle!" said Nell's dad, mangling another saying. Nell's mum rolled her eyes – she'd probably heard plenty similarly mangled sayings over the years.

"Nope, I managed to avoid the Bermuda Triangle, thanks – I just got stuck in traffic on the way back from the supermarket. Anyway, you must be Kezzy!"

I nodded as I squeezed water out of the ends of my plaits.

"I'm Marianne. You haven't been here long, then? I thought you were maybe coming straight from school, and would be dying for tea by now!"

"Um, no – I went home and got changed and did my homework first," I explained as Nell's smiley mum shared her bags out between Nell and her dad and let them carry them away.

"Nell's been telling us all about your parents," said Marianne, slipping off her North Face jacket to reveal . . . a plain T-shirt, jeans and those sort of trendy hill-walking trainer-shoes. Nell was right about her mother dressing like she was about to go hiking. "I love the sound of your mum's hobby! Bibi, isn't it? I wish I had the patience to be as creative as her!"

I thought of the woollen fish that Mum was busy with last night; just one piece of the under-the-sea mobile she was knitting to hang above the baby's cot. Right at this second, in this warm, welcoming and seemingly sane house, I wondered if knitting fish was better described as creative or just plain *nuts*.

"Well. . ." I said vaguely, with a shy smile and a shrug.

"Want to come through to the TV room?" asked Nell, arriving back with a couple of cans of something fizzy for us.

"I'll give you a shout when tea's ready!" Nell's mum smiled, not at all put out by my shyness, or Nell cutting short our conversation.

"Irn Bru – time you tasted it!" said Nell, nodding at the can as I followed her through into a large white-painted room with vast, dark-red leather sofas and a matching blood-red wall where an ornate fireplace stood.

"Wow!" I muttered at the room's sleek, newly decorated poshness.

Spotting that I was about to sink into one of the sofas, Nell shook her head and nodded at me to follow her. "Through *here*!"

The red room had a TV in it, but apparently wasn't the TV room. That instead turned out to be the room through the interconnecting glass doors.

Nell flumped into a slightly tatty, squashy, olive-green sofa instead and pointed out the matching chair and footstool for me to sit on.

"*This* feels like home!" she said with a laugh, as she yanked at the ring pull and quickly glugged the orange bubbles frothing from the top of the open can. "The stuff in this room is ancient – it's been in every flat and house we've ever lived in!"

I liked this room – worn, comfy furniture that easily gave the (fake) impression that it had been in this particular house for ever. A big, old non-flat-screen telly in the corner, and a chunky coffee table with scratches and occasional pen marks on it; everything here seemed well used and well loved. I guess wherever Nell's family moved to, this stuff helped make her feel at home straight away.

"Awww . . . don't I look cute?"

Nell was pulling a face and pointing to a huge, blown-up photo on the wall of both Nell's parents laughing, with a gap-toothed mini-version of Nell getting cuddled to bits in between them.

"How old were you?" I asked. The image reminded me of a much less glam, far more ordinary, but just as cutely-cosy photo of me, Mum and Dad on the dodgem cars at the fair when I was four or five.

"Six, I think."

Looking at the picture and sipping my Irn Bru (it was pretty good), I realized something that was a) true and b) a bit corny, so I stayed just thinking it and didn't say it out loud. But what I was thinking was that me and Nell were both pretty lucky, having sickeningly nice parents who we happened to get along with really well. I mean, plenty of people I knew had mums and dads they argued with and didn't get on with much at all.

Yep, we were both mega-lucky.

"Do you think our parents would like each other?" Nell suddenly asked, maybe thinking along similar-ish lines to me.

"Maybe!" I answered with a shrug, picturing Nell's dad joking around with mine, and Mum trying to persuade "Marianne" that the best way to get to know new people in her new neighbourhood was to pick up a pair of knitting needles and cast on alongside the likes of Sheila and Mrs Laskaris and Gabrielle (and her dropped stitches and swearing) of a Saturday morning.

"We should do something for them! A good deed for our parents!" Nell suddenly suggested, her eyes wide and her voice lowered.

"Like what?" It was a nice idea, but what kind of cool surprise could we land on our folks?

"Maybe. . ." But Nell seemed stumped all of a sudden, even though she'd come up with the basic notion in the first place.

"*I* know!" I exclaimed in a sudden low, undercover voice. "This weekend we should just try really, really hard to be interested in them! Y'know, to ask them stuff about when *they* were young and everything. Adults *always* get a big kick out of kids being interested in their pasts!"

I'd thought about that last Saturday, when I remembered about Mum and her original tattoo. She *must* have told me once upon a time what was there before. . . I'd have to ask her again. *And* get her to tell me all the cool places she'd travelled to when she was young. As for Dad, I definitely remembered once seeing a scuzzy, hand-held old video tape of him when he was surfing (i.e., he was a wobbly dark splodge on a distant wave), but I could ask him to dig it out again. I was sure it would give him a buzz. . .

"God, yeah! Brilliant idea!" Nell said enthusiastically, staring at the blown-up photo on the wall. I could practically hear her mind racing from where I was sitting.

"Well, let's try and do this tomorrow, then we can meet on Sunday and see how we got on," I suggested. "And if we're *both* doing stuff for *both* our parents, we should have lots to write up in the Karma Club book."

"*Definitely.* Anyway, we haven't done any secret good deeds since we gave Miss Lennard the apple on Tuesday, so it would be great to have something else, like, something really *major*, to write down in there."

That's when I remembered.

I'd never really forgotten, if I was being honest.

Since Wednesday, the knowledge of what I'd done had been nipping at my conscience like the Ugly Barky Dog.

Not that I really expected Nell to mind; I mean, wasn't the Karma Club all about being as kind and as nice as you could be, even if the person you were being kind to hadn't a clue who'd done the good deed? Or, um, even if the person you were being kind to didn't one hundred per cent *deserve* the good deed?

"I, uh . . . I've written something new down in here, actually," I said, taking the gold notebook out of my hoodie pocket. At the same time, I quickly checked over my shoulder for any signs of parents in the vicinity.

"Oh, *yeah*?!" laughed Nell, leaning forward while I wasn't looking and snatching the book clean out of my hand. "What secret mission have you been on, then?"

The Tenth Secret: it was about to be revealed. I needn't have worried; Nell would be fine with this. One hundred and ten per cent fine. I was a thousand per cent sure.

I watched, my heart pitter-patter-POUNDING, as Nell flicked to the newest, scribbled-on page and silently read.

Oh.

Her beaming smile miniaturized in front of my very eyes, till it was hardly there at all.

Uh-oh.

She had to be reading what I'd written again, as Nell wasn't exactly a slow reader, and should have been done by now.

The olive of the slouchy sofa seemed to intensify, till it filled the room with a glowing green vapour. If I wanted to make up a smell to go with the imaginary vapour I could sense, I'd guess it might be poisonous, not unlike gas mixed with fox wee. (Nasty.)

"Why did you do it?"

At Nell's simple question, I deflated. It was, of course, the stupidest idea I'd ever had.

"I just . . . I just thought . . . well, it would be a sweet thing to do, for old time's sake, I suppose," I garbled and shrugged, and shrugged and garbled.

It had made some kind of sense, I think, when I'd gone into the chemist's on Wednesday after school –

when Nell had met up with her mum to go shopping – and bought the tiny pink pig with the yellow buttercup flowers dotted on it.

It had made some kind of sense when I bought the wrapping paper, padded envelope and birthday card from Mr Patel's, and written the card and the envelope out anonymously, using a dumb, half-broken alphabet stencil that I'd found in my pencil case, just so that Tara wouldn't recognize my writing.

It had made some kind of sense when I took the whole lot to the post office on the high street, and imagined Tara's face on Saturday when she opened the present.

Maybe she'd figure out that it was me. Maybe I didn't *want* it to stay secret. Maybe I wanted Tara to realize that I was a fantastic friend who she hadn't appreciated. Maybe I wanted her to feel just a little bit sorry and sad that she didn't have me as a best friend any more.

I guess I hadn't really thought how my *new* best friend might feel about all of that.

"I just don't see how you could *do* that, Kezzy!" Nell snapped at me, sounding – and looking – pretty cut-up. "As far as I've seen, that Tara girl hasn't ever been nice to you *or* your mum!"

Or *Audrey*, I suddenly remembered, thinking of Tara's sniggers that day when the First Secret of the Karma Club had happened – along with the bike accident – in the park.

"I just sort of thought that—"

"And how could you keep it secret from me?" Nell interrupted angrily. "What's the point in *that*?"

"I didn't really think about it. . ."

I might as well have slapped her in the face. That last bit came out *so* wrong, making me sound as if I cared zero per cent about what Nell thought, but there was no chance to bumble on and make it sound better.

"Say hello to . . . PIZZA!!" Nell's mum called out from the doorway, giant plates of steaming-hot pizza in both hands, while Nell's dad was in the background shouting, "And dips! Don't forget the chips and dips, Marianne!"

Party food. How perfect for my personal I-Messed-Up party. . .

The Eleventh Secret

"Mum, *tell* me."

"I already have!" Mum laughed, putting her knitting needles and brown woolly tree creation to one side so she could go and answer the door.

"Yeah, yeah . . . so it was a heart. But it must have been a very *wonky* heart for you to cover it up with a great big tattoo of a sunflower!"

"It was a terrible, *very* wonky heart – you're right," Mum's voice called back as she waddled along the hall. "Oh, hi, Sheila, come on in!"

Sheila from the Rebel Knitters' Society: Mum had said she was popping round on Sunday morning to borrow Mum's pattern for an Arran-cardie-style hot-water-bottle cover (what *else*?!).

Well, if Mum was busy (and, of course, Sheila would stay for a cup of tea and probably a quick knit), I'd go and bug Dad instead.

He was out in the shed. That's the old-fashioned cliché of what dads are meant to do, isn't it? Hang out in the shed, listening to the sports results on the radio while fixing or making things. So here was my modern-day dad with his radio on (tuned to a station playing some old reggae classic), and he was making something for sure, only nothing that fitted the old cliché, like shelves or whatever.

Oh, no.

Dad was making lots of half-a-bees.

Sixteen of them, to be precise.

"What was so wrong with Mum's heart?" I asked him, hovering at the open shed door and watching him covering up yet another small plastic milk carton in gloopy papier maché (the first part of the bees), ready to take into nursery next day for the kids to paint black and yellow stripes on (the finishing touch). Of course, the kids would end up with it all on themselves too. Joe and all his tiddly mates would finish their session looking like they were imitating our horrible school uniform, in poster paint.

"What?!" asked Dad, confused and slightly anxious.

He'd been getting more jumpy around Mum recently, practically hyperventilating if she so much as sneezed or sighed a bit. But I guess it was because the weeks were ticking away and there were only six to go now till our family got a quarter bigger.

"The heart she was talking about last night!" I told him, tapping my arm where it corresponded with Mum's tattoos, old and new.

Last night had been fun, actually. Instead of putting on a movie, like we usually did, I'd asked Mum and Dad if we could do other stuff instead, like look at old photos and videos of them.

My parents seemed touched and pleased that I'd asked – not to mention slightly giddy. They giggled more than *me* at the sight of Dad's long hair, during the ten-minute section (that we fast-forwarded through) of him waxing his pet surfboard.

As for Mum's hair, it was much the same pinned-up

style as now, only in her jumbled box of old photos, you could see it was twisted into cornrows which *eventually* turned to dreads by the end of her travels. And in every photo – from the outback of Australia to the temples of India, from the south coast of France to the rice paddies of Vietnam, from the Golden Gate Bridge in San Francisco to the Great Wall of China – Mum had the same red-and-white checked scarf tied around it.

"It must have *stunk!*" we'd teased her, me and Dad.

"I *washed* it!" Mum had protested, but I don't know if we were that convinced.

As we laughed and joked and teased and ate home-made popcorn, I felt pleased that the Eleventh Secret of the Karma Club was going so well, specially since I'd made such a mess of the Tenth. But I tried hard to put that to the back of my mind, so I could do the best job I could.

It pinged to the *front* of my mind while I lay in bed that night, though. Nell's hurt/confused/angry expression kept coming into sharp focus every time I turned over and tried to go to sleep. As I tossed and turned and tossed some more, I found myself wondering if the Karma Club was even going to exist for much longer. I mean, I spoke more to Nell's parents than *her* over tea, and felt so awkward about the whole Tara/pig present disaster that I pretended I needed to get home early.

Yeah, get home early, so I could kick myself in the privacy of my own room. . ..

"Oh, you mean Mum's old heart *tattoo!*" said Dad with a sigh of relief, now that he realized I was talking about a piece of bad artwork rather than a medical condition when I'd asked what was wrong with her heart.

"Well, *yeah*. So what was so wrong with it? Did *you* think it looked bad?"

"I didn't ever see it – she had the sunflower by the time *I* met her."

Oh. I didn't realize that Mum had already moved on to Phase Two of her tattoo by the time she hitched up in Cornwall.

"By the way, while we're on the subject, can I tell you something?" said Dad, putting down a half-a-bee and looking at me very earnestly. The last time he'd looked at me like that and sounded so serious, he and Mum had launched into the whole facts-of-life talk. Urgh . . . was there a Phase Two of the facts-of-life talk that I didn't know about?

"Of course," I said warily.

"It's a secret – a *big* secret. Something your mum doesn't know."

OK, so it wasn't anything to do with the facts of life, then. Mum knew pretty much all about them, or she wouldn't be having a baby in a few weeks' time.

"Go on," I urged him, thinking of the gold notebook upstairs in my room that was packed with secrets.

"I love Bibi. I love her style. I love all her mad knitting, even the covers she knitted for my speakers."

Actually, that was a bit of a fib. I knew Dad absolutely adored his wood-framed, vintage, 1970s hi-fi speakers and that it took a lot for him to hide them under the "fun" covers that Mum had made for his fortieth birthday last year. (His face that day gave it away; the bottom half had a smile slapped on, but his eyes were flashing, "Eeek! *Noooooo!!*")

"Uh-huh," I mumbled, wondering what was coming next.

"But the thing is, I'm not that wild about her tattoo. I don't really like tattoos at *all*. . ."

"Really?" I said, genuinely surprised. Mum wore vest tops and vest dresses all summer long and so had her sunflower on show a lot of the time. I had no idea that Dad wasn't a fan of it.

But you know, what really freaked me out was the idea of my parents having secrets – even fairly minor ones – from each other. It just didn't seem right; as unlikely as ever seeing my mum wearing a short, neat hairstyle and a power suit.

"Really," said Dad, looking a bit shamefaced by his confession. "Don't tell her, though – I don't want to hurt her feelings. And I know she only did the sunflower to cover up the first one, which she regretted getting done in the first place."

It had been a whim when she was travelling, she'd said last night. A mad, bad idea that had popped into her head, when she was unfortunately in the vicinity of a tattoo parlour. I guess it was a bit like that time when my fringe was too long and bugging me, and there just happened to be a pair of scissors on the bathroom shelf. In both cases, the results were rubbish, but at least mine wasn't *permanent*.

"I promise I won't te—"

"KEZZY!" Mum's voice yelled from the house. "VISITOR FOR YOOOOU!!"

I stepped out of the shed, and saw . . . Nell.

She was coming out of the back door, smiling kind of ruefully at me. She waved her fingers at me. I waved mine back and began to walk towards her, my heart soaring.

Nell rubbed her fingers at the edge of the waistcoat she was wearing over her T-shirt, to show me where her gold heart was. With a grin, I spun around and pointed at my bottom, or at least at the left-hand back pocket of my jeans where my own gold heart was pinned.

Phew – looked like we were both still members of the Karma Club, then.

As if we were some kind of landlocked synchronized swimmers, me and Nell found ourselves aiming – in unison – in the direction of the crumbly old wooden bench parked under the kitchen window. We'd be risking splinters here, but it was worth it, in the circumstances. I mean, what were a couple of agonizing splinters in the thigh compared to nearly losing a strong and sparkly friendship?

"You all right?" I asked, bursting with happiness at the sight of Nell, especially a Nell that wasn't looking confused, hurt or angry this time.

"Yeah," she said with a shrug. "Look, I'm sorry about . . . getting all mad at you on Friday night, over sending that present and everything."

"No – *I'm* sorry! I shouldn't have done it; it was a dumb idea, and I kind of half-knew it when I was doing it. I just felt a bit weird, thinking it was Tara's birthday and how we used to be so close, and. . ."

". . .and *I* felt a bit weird," Nell jumped in, explaining

herself in the gap when I was struggling to set everything straight, "'cause I thought I'd made a fool of myself. Y'know, thinking we were best mates, when really, Tara was still your best mate, in a way."

"But she's not!" I insisted.

"Yeah, I realize that *now* – it just didn't seem that way when you started talking about the pig. . ."

We both suddenly looked at each other, aware of how ridiculous that sounded. How completely daft that we'd nearly put our friendship in jeopardy over a stupid pink pig, covered in stupid yellow buttercups!

We found ourselves lost in ripples of giggles, sniggering at the ridiculousness of it all, as well as through relief and not a *little* bit of nerves.

"Anyway, how did your side of the parent project go?" hissed Nell, getting back to business after our temporary glitch.

"Good!" I said with a nod. "What about you?"

"Yep, good too! Let's go upstairs to your room. . ."

I knew what she meant – our garden wasn't very big, and even though Dad was currently yelling along to some old reggae track, he might've been able to catch bits of what we were saying when the DJ came back on.

We got up – amazingly splinter-free – grabbed some juice and biscuits from the kitchen, and were about to head up the stairs when Mum called out to me from the living room. Well, called out to *Nell,* actually.

"Nell, what are your parents' names again?" she asked as we hovered in the living-room doorway.

"Um, Marianne and John," she answered.

"Ah, yes. Anyway, the thing is, we're going to have a barbecue here next Saturday afternoon," said Mum, glancing up from the sofa, with her unidentified tree-thing growing from her knitting needles. Sheila was sitting on one of the armchairs, smiling benevolently as she click-clacked in a lightning blur.

"*Are* we?" I frowned at Mum. It was the first *I'd* heard of it.

"Yes," said Mum, very definitely. "I just decided two minutes ago. I realized I'd really like to have a bit of a party before I get any bigger, and I probably won't have the energy for ages after the baby's born!"

I shrugged and smiled. It seemed like a perfectly ace idea to me.

"So anyway, Nell, I just wondered if you and Marianne and John might like to come?"

Nell never looked shy (that was more *my* job), but she certainly blushed at Mum's invite. That's when it dawned on me that no matter how confident and funny she seemed, it must be hard to always be the new girl. No wonder she'd felt so insecure because of my truly *useless* idea of sending the pig to Tara. . .

"Yes, yes – I'm sure they'd be up for it!" Nell nodded. "And me too, of course!"

"I'll bring potato salad," Sheila chipped in.

So the rebel knitters would be out in force, I thought, cluttering up our smallish garden with their lethal needles!

"Oh, and I meant to say, Kezzy," Sheila added, turning her attention away from potato salad to me, "guess who came into my charity shop yesterday afternoon?"

I wasn't in the mood for guessing games. Not 'cause I was in an impatient or grumpy mood or anything; just the opposite. My mind was skipping around too much with the happiness of having Nell back that trying to get it to concentrate was like trying to get a bunch of butterflies to sit still in a neat line.

"I don't know," I said, after pretending to mull over Sheila's question for a second.

"Your nice friend Tara!"

Thunk.

That was the sound of my happiness fizzling away to nothing. Even the smile slipped from Sheila's face as she realized that she'd said something that didn't appear to be all that fantastic.

"Tara's more of an *old* friend now," Mum jumped in and explained. "Kezzy doesn't really see so much of her since she switched schools."

"Oh! Oh, right!" said Sheila, trying to gauge what the situation was. "Well, I, um, was just going to say it was very funny, because she and her mum came in yesterday with boxes and boxes of *pigs*, would you believe! They said they were having a clear-out, as it was Tara's birthday, and she was getting rid of all her more babyish things. But *pigs*! I just couldn't believe it when I saw how many piggy things there were in those boxes!"

I could, having seen them at close quarters. And at the top of one of the boxes would be a brand-new pig who'd picked the wrong time to join the litter.

Even though she'd forgiven me, I couldn't have blamed Nell if she felt a little smug at the idea of my secret present being unwrapped and almost immediately thrown away. But I don't think she *did* feel smug – at least if she did, she hid it pretty well. All I knew was that out of sight of Mum and Sheila, she was giving my hand a quick squeeze.

"Hey, Kezzy – weren't we going to hurry and do that thing?" Nell said brightly, bailing me out of an uncomfortable situation with one of her convincing but vague excuses.

"Mmm! Yes! Er . . . bye!" I muttered with a nod and a wave.

I bumbled out of the door, knowing my face was probably as pink as the little pottery pig that was now languishing in the charity shop window.

"Thanks," I whispered to Nell, as we hurriedly padded up the stairs.

"You're welcome," said Nell, smiling at me over her shoulder. "And before you ask, the thing we're going to do . . . it's this: make a vow *never* to mention pigs again! Yeah?"

Oink, oink to that. . .

The Twelfth Secret

"BARK! BARK! BARK! BARK! BARK! BARK! BAR—"

Slam!!

Even with my bedroom window firmly shut, I could tell that the Ugly Barky Dog was still barking because. . .

a) I could – unfortunately – still hear it, though more faintly, thanks to the double glazing, and because . . .

b) I'd just watched some teenagers pass its house and leap away terrified as it hurled itself in their direction, only being stopped by the ornate metal bars of the gate.

"I always used to nag at my parents for a puppy," said Nell, her feet up on my window seat, pinging M&Ms up in the air and catching them in her mouth. "But I'm kind of glad they said no now. I mean, what if it grew up to be ugly and barky and unpopular like that one?"

"Nah, that could never happen," I replied, idly flicking through the magazine on my lap. "There couldn't be *two* such ugly, barky, unpopular dogs in the world!"

What a difference a week makes. At 6.45 p.m. last

Friday, I had wild indigestion and was trying to suss out a way of leaving Nell's, and leaving the bad atmosphere (colour: navy blue) I'd helped to create.

Today at the same time, we were lounging in my room post-tea, chilling out, fooling around and laughing at a magazine feature about the blob-shaped babies of beautiful celebrities – just like the absolute best friends we were. (The mood was coloured apricot, in case you wanted to know.)

Actually, after last week's blip, me and Nell were closer than ever. Maybe we needed a small buttercup-covered pig to come between us, so we could both appreciate each other a bit more. I don't know. But whatever, we were fine; a whole lot *better* than fine, in fact.

A red M&M spun up in the air . . . Nell opened wide to catch it . . . and missed.

PLOP! went the sweet, landing on the cover of the gold notebook as if it were just another shiny plastic jewel.

"We should think up another good deed," said Nell, nodding at the notebook as she quickly picked up the M&M and popped it in her mouth.

True . . . we hadn't written anything in it since Saturday. The last entry had been in two sets of handwriting. Mine said, "*Made Mum and Dad laugh. Mum showing photos of her backpacking trip and all the mates she made on the way, Dad trying to hide photos of the terrible long hairdo he once had!*" Nell's said, "*Asked Dad to play me music he liked at my age – we were dancing to Madness and the Boomtown Rats till 11 p.m.! And got Mum to show us some salsa moves, from when she used to go to classes (she even wore a dress!). P.S. Didn't know you could salsa to ska and punk music, but you can!"*

We'd been a good-deed-free zone ever since. Maybe we were just tired out, since the Tenth Secret of the Karma Club had been lousy and the Eleventh had been so successful. Whatever . . . neither of us had rushed to suggest anything that might become the Twelfth Secret of the Karma Club.

I flicked through the magazine pages again, thinking about nothing much in particular. And there was the page again, with the non-attractive children of famously gorgeous parents.

"Do you think that it's some weird genetic thing?" I asked Nell. "You know; two very good-looking people make ugly kids? Or do you think the kids will eventually grow out of the ugly stage and grow into beautiful beings?"

"Darling, you're being *sooo* shallow," said Nell, goofing around. "Don't you know, 'beauty comes from within'?"

Beauty comes from within.

Well, so do ideas, and I was having one now. . .

We were in cagoules again, our hoods up once more, but we weren't doing anything involving buckets of soapy water and sponges this time.

Nope – the Twelfth Secret of the Karma Club involved a leftover lamb and rosemary sausage and hand-knitted red ribbon.

"BARK! BARK! BA—"

Dogs are so predictable. One sniff of a sausage and they stop in their tracks.

The Ugly Barky Dog's nose was going into overdrive, wibbling frantically at the blatant bribe we'd snuck over with.

"Are we cool?" I asked, on my knees, eye level with the Ugly Barky Dog's snout and its ugly, toothy overbite. I'd never been so close to it before, mainly because its ear-splitting barks were a serious health hazard to the general public's hearing.

"We're cool," said Nell, glancing up and down my quietish street, and peeking too at the windows of the Ugly Barky Dog's house. (I was worried that his bland bald owner might come out at any second, concerned by the strange and unnatural sound of silence coming from his garden. . .)

"Good dog!" I whispered, gently opening the gate and slipping, on my haunches, inside.

The Ugly Barky Dog couldn't make up its mind whether to pay more attention to me or the sausage, but surprisingly (and reassuringly) it didn't seem to want to eat me. It was doing a lot of staring, but then I guess it was used to people backing away at the twin horrors of its general ugliness and noise.

"*Very* good dog!" I repeated, as it gently took the sausage from my fingers, leaving me free to pull the long knitted red ribbon out of my cagoule pocket. It was the one Mum had tied round her hair in a big floppy bow a couple of weeks ago. But she'd left it by the bin, ready to throw out, after she'd spotted a dropped stitch in it, and had already knitted three more in different colours.

"Here . . . let's see what *this* looks like," I said softly, tying the floppy red bow around Ugly Barky Dog's neck. He didn't resist. But as I tied, I felt a small, cold metal disc brush against the back of my hand. I grabbed hold of it and read one side: an address and phone number. On the other side . . . "Buddy". Ugly Barky Dog's name was *Buddy*? That was a pretty friendly name for a pretty unfriendly dog.

"Aww! It looks so *cute*!" whispered Nell, kneeling down to join me, but on the other side of the gate. "I can't believe how sweet it looks with that big bow on! And aw . . . check out his big, brown eyes gazing up at us!"

"He's called Buddy," I told her. "Funny name for a dog who frightens everyone all the time!"

The "frightening" Ugly Barky Dog dropped what was left of the sausage and gave me a lick.

"Hey! His tail! It's going mental!!"

Nell was right – it was. Buddy could have been doing an impression of a canine helicopter, the way his tail was whizzing round in circles at high speed.

"Maybe he was just always trying to get people's attention with all that barking, just to be matey. . ." I mused out loud.

"Hold it! A light's come on in the hall!" Nell hissed.

Time to retreat. Fast. With a pat on his spiky head, I crawled backwards out of Buddy's garden, and pulled the gate silently closed. Then me and Nell ran, bent double, along the pavement, across the road and into my house laughing – remembering at the last minute to pull off our disguises (the cagoules) and bundle them into balls in our hands.

"What's going on?" Mum yelled from the kitchen, where we could see her sitting the wrong way round in a chair, getting her back massaged by Dad.

"Nothing! Nell's just being silly!" I called back, as we giggled our way up the stairs and hurtled to our perfect vantage point at my bedroom window.

"*Quick!*" I urged Nell, getting there first.

It couldn't be better. Not only was the (Cute) Ugly Barky Dog's owner on his path, scratching his head, but Harassed Single Mum was standing on the pavement by the open gate, her hands on her hips and laughing at the sight of this comically cute dog in his red ribbon, parading up and down the pavement as her bundle of delighted kids cooed over him.

"It's a three-starrer!" announced Nell, picking up the notebook and her gold pen.

"Let's celebrate!" I laughed, grabbing the bag of M&Ms and tossing one into the air.

Nell caught it in her mouth mid-giggle and nearly choked – which made us even more hysterical.

"Erm, are you two sure you're all right?!" asked Mum, suddenly peering round the slightly open bedroom door.

Nell squealed and quickly sat on the notebook, which made us snigger uncontrollably.

After a couple of minutes of seeing that we couldn't stop and weren't about to make any sense, Mum gave up and left the secret members of the secret Karma Club to their very silly secrets. . .

The Thirteenth Secret

Bad karma.

You wouldn't have been able to see it coming . . . not this Saturday afternoon, not with the Mediterranean blue of the sky and the mellow yellow of the sun.

And the smiles, infectious smiles a mile wide, from Mum to Dad and back again. Those smiles didn't signal any bad karma on the way. Not to *me*, anyway, watching them as I ran about with paper plates and jugs of juice, sneaking proud peeks at my parents and thinking, yet again, how lucky I was to be one chunk of this small-but-perfectly-formed family.

Mum: she was looking gorgeous in a rose-pink cotton vest dress with soft ruffles at the hem (yes, of *course* knitted). To go with it she'd knitted a myriad of tiny pink rosebuds that she'd clipped in her hair, and even wore rose-pink knitted laces in her trainers. The outfit was matched by the healthy rose-pink glow in the cheeks of her lightly sun-kissed face.

"You're *beautiful*, Bibi!" Dad told her for the umpteenth time, leaning over from the barbecue to grab a kiss from her, a protective, loving hand on her bump, the other hand holding a pair of barbecue tongs in the air out of harm's way.

My parents' happiness was infectious. Quite a few

people were milling around in our garden, though the party had only officially started about ten minutes ago, and all of them were smiling and laughing too. There were Mum and Dad's regular friends, their work friends, a smattering of Rebel Knitters (Sheila and Elzbieta had snaffled the bench and were comparing knitting stitches between sips of wine), plus a few neighbours too.

There was no sign of Nell or her parents yet, but it was pretty early. And as I'd appointed myself the door monitor, I'd moved the mobile bell unit to the kitchen windowsill, so I wouldn't miss Nell – or anyone else – when they ding-donged.

Ding-dong!

"I got it!" I yelled, zooming through the house.

"Um, hello!" said a woman on the doorstep, with a gaggle of kids hiding behind her. She was wearing a loose top and cropped trousers and looked like the Harassed Single Mum's much prettier, more relaxed twin sister. "I'm here for the party . . . Neil invited me at nursery the other day?"

"Oh! Yeah! Come on in!" I bumbled awkwardly, feeling myself flush at such a close-up view of our neighbours (large and small). Dad hadn't said anything about asking them along today, but then why would he? He wasn't to know that I had a particular (secret) interest or two in this particular family. "I'm Kezzy, by the way. . ."

"I'm Sonia," said the mum, ushering her brood in front of her. "And this is Maisie . . . Bella . . . Joe, and the littlest one's Danny."

"I've met Joe already," I told her, as Joe lifted his

head and gave me a tiny smile, just visible despite the thumb in his mouth. "I met him when I helped out at the nursery a couple of weeks ago. . ."

"Oh, right! I think I remember seeing you there!" said Sonia, studying my face for recognition. "He's really settled in there now."

"Yeah . . . great. Um, do you just want to go straight out to the garden? I'll bring out some crisps and popcorn and stuff for the kids."

As they shuffled through the kitchen and out into the bustling garden, I busied myself in the kitchen. I didn't need to, as there were already plenty of kiddy-friendly snacks dotted around on surfaces outside. I just had to catch my breath for a second, to get over the surprise at the sudden introduction to Sonia and Co, and to work out why I now felt so overpoweringly *anxious*.

Was it just too weird having a couple of "secrets" come zooming into my personal space? Did it maybe feel like I was somehow about to be found out?

Hey, I was acting all paranoid, getting things out of proportion.

I just needed a way of calming myself down, and getting the frantic butterflies flapping around in my chest to sit down in that imaginary line I was fixing in my mind.

Ah, I had it; I'd think of all the Karma Club secrets so far . . . recite them list-style in my head like a mantra. And anyway, Nell would be here any minute, with her usual enthusiasm radiating out like a blinding white aura, and I'd be fine, and ready to party.

In the meantime. . .

The Secrets of the Karma Club
1) The Karma Club coming into existence
2) The Karma Club being a secret
3) Giving Glen the hot chocolate
4) Hand-delivering the thank-you letter to Mr Patel
5) Planting sunflowers in Audrey's window box
6) Scribbling good graffiti over bad
7) Washing the Harassed Single Mum's car for her
8) Joe the Shy Kid getting a Smarties smile
9) Sneaking an apple to our teacher
10) The dumb birthday pig. . . (the less said – and thought – about that, the better)
11) Listening to our parents' past glories
12) Doing a makeover on the Ugly Barky Dog.

There. I felt calmer already. And what, I found myself wondering as I emptied popcorn in a big mixing bowl, would the Thirteenth Secret of the Karma Club be?

I stopped, mid-empty.

Thirteen wasn't exactly the *luckiest* number in the world. Well, maybe it was as pleasant as twelve and fourteen in places like Tanzania and Iceland and Sri Lanka; I didn't know for sure. But what I *did* know was that here in Britain, the number thirteen was all tangled up with superstitions about bad luck and trouble. . .

Ding-dong!

Good: I was saved from thinking dark, dumb thoughts by the bell.

"Hi! Is this where the barbecue's happening?"

I *think* that's what the bald man on the doorstep was saying, but he was more-than-slightly drowned out by the bark-bark-barking of his dog.

"Yeah, yeah it is!" I said, bending down and patting Buddy, and at the same time inspecting Secret Number Twelve, which was looking good. The knitted ribbon was still in place, with the bow worn at a rakish angle.

At the friendly touch of my hand, Buddy stopped his yapping and switched to happy panting instead. His tail was doing the frantic helicopter whirl again.

"Sorry – Buddy always gets a bit overexcited," the man apologized as I ushered him inside. "By the way, you don't have any cats, do you? He goes completely *doolally* when it comes to cats. I forgot to ask Bibi when she invited me. . ."

Mum and Dad had been busy, asking lesser-known neighbours along to our little party, like Sonia and the bald bloke, whose name I didn't know yet. Hey, maybe my parents had a little secret of their own, being matchmakers? After all, I'd never seen the bland, bald bloke with a wife since he moved in. . .

Actually, I couldn't really see Sonia and the bald bloke together, but it made me smile anyway, thinking of Buddy and the little kids all rolling around together, like one big, happy litter of puppies.

"No, there're no cats," I assured him, then spotted someone – *three* someones – coming up the front path. "Um, just go straight through!"

"That was *Buddy*?" Nell whispered excitedly, bounding forward for a quick, private word before her parents caught her up.

She was dressed much like me, I noticed, in a floaty, cool skirt and a T-shirt. Her mum was decked out in her usual hiking-style outfit, only with a pendant sort of necklace to dress it up. Nell's dad looked more relaxed than when I'd seen him last; he was suit-free, but still looking smart-ish in neatly ironed jeans and a linen short-sleeved shirt.

"Yeah!" I giggled to Nell. "Mum asked his owner to the party. Spooky, huh? And you'll never *guess* who else is here. . ."

But I didn't get to the Harassed Single Mum and her kid Joe and Co – she'd just have to spot them herself.

"Hi, Kezzy!" Nell's dad said breezily. "We come armed with gifts!"

"John, you're making it sound like we brought frankincense and myrrh!" joked Nell's mum. "It's just a quiche, and some wine, and flowers."

"*I* chose the flowers!" Nell said with a grin, pointing to the paper-wrapped bunch of sunflowers.

Was that a sly reference to Secret Number Five? I wondered, heading into the house.

"Nell's been going on about how beautiful your mum's tattoo is," said Nell's mum, following me.

OK, so *that's* what Nell meant.

"Come and I'll introduce you, and you can see it for yourself!" I told her, leading everyone out of the duskiness of the house and into the chattery noise and brightness of our garden.

But I couldn't see Mum straight away; she was lost in conversation somewhere in the throng of guests milling around our small patch of grass and slightly overgrown shrubs. Still, there was someone *else* I could introduce them to.

"Dad – this is John and Marianne, Nell's parents!"

Dad came out from behind the barbecue, in his party outfit of a clean T-shirt, baggy grey combats, bare feet and a knitted butcher's style stripy apron.

He swapped the tongs around in his hands and held the right one out to do some shaking.

"Pleased to meet you!" he beamed at them. "Bibi and I are really glad you could come. You'll meet her in a second – can't miss her, really!"

"Looking forward to it!" Marianne said, smiling warmly in return. "Nell just talks non-stop about you two and the house. I think our place is a bit of a let-down to her after a visit to yours!"

"All Bibi's work, nothing to do with me," Dad laughed. "She'll give you the guided tour when she shows up!"

"Er, we don't have to pay, do we?" Nell's dad joked.

I didn't notice that me and Nell were holding hands till she squeezed mine, chuffed – as I was – that our parents had hit it off so easily, so quickly.

Maybe they'll feel like forever friends straight away, same as me and Nell? I thought, my heart soaring with possibilities.

How strange to think that at *that* moment, I had absolutely no idea that the Thirteenth Secret of the Karma Club was *almost* ready to reveal itself, and when it did, it was going to feel like I'd just been *punched. . .*

"Nope, but you'll have to be careful, Marianne,"

Dad continued, wafting the tongs at Nell's mum, "or she'll have you signing up to the Rebel Knitters' Society before you know it!"

"Well, you know, I might just enjoy th—"

"Oh, speak of the devil, here she is now!" Dad interrupted, as Mum melted through the relaxed throng of partygoers to appear by our side, like a rose-pink apparition.

"What have you been saying about me now, Neil?" she smiled at him.

"Only *fantastic* things, honey. Anyway, Nell and her folks are here . . . this is Marianne, and this is John. And this of course is—"

"Belinda!" burst out Nell's dad.

"*John?!*" said Mum, who virtually *no one* knew as Belinda.

A long, long, confused silence followed, which probably only lasted about half a second. But it was half a second when the world took on a strange, unearthly glow, like the time when I was nine and there was a daytime eclipse. It was a bizarre, hazy half-light, as if someone had thrown gauze over your face and asked you to stare at the world through it.

I felt the claustrophobia of the gauze descending now, and didn't understand what it was. But it was something to do with Nell's dad using Mum's long-lost real name, combined with Dad's confused expression, mixed in with the fact that Nell's mum's mouth had just dropped open in shock.

"You . . . you look . . . *exactly* the same!" Nell's dad blurted out.

"And you look *completely* different!" Mum laughed, though the smile on her face wasn't totally convincing.

"What's going on?" Nell whispered, either in actual words or telepathically, I couldn't tell in the confusion of the moment.

"What's going on?" I said out loud, ignoring the shy side that wanted to curl up and hide from whatever weirdness was happening.

"Well, this is . . . I mean. . ." Mum fumbled, smiling at me sweetly, apologetically. "The thing is . . . well, I used to be married to John."

Instant musical statues: that's what our two families were playing. Musical statues with the added extra element of forgetting to *breathe*.

"Belinda!" Nell's dad burst out in a gale of laughter that didn't sound very funny. "You still *are*!"

Bad karma, pleased to meet you. . .

The Fourteenth Secret

It was funny, it really was.

What am I talking about? Well, me being so surprised last week at the idea of *Dad* keeping a secret from *Mum*.

Of course, Mum's secret was *planet*-sized in comparison. Dad's dislike of tattoos turned into a big "so what?" next to *that* not-so-little gem.

Mind you, I found out last night that Dad had kept part of his tattoo-confession a secret from me . . . he hadn't ever seen it, but he'd known all along that Mum's original, terrible, *wonky* tattoo had read "*I* ♥ *John*".

It turned out that *way* back when they first got together in Cornwall, Mum had told Dad that she'd had the tattoo done in the US, in a moment of madness, in honour of some boyfriend she'd been crazy about for all of two minutes. The sunflower cover-up had happened a few months later, in Amsterdam, with the luckily small heart and the boyfriend's name getting easily covered over by the brown centre of the flower.

So Dad knew. He just didn't know Mum had ever *married* the boyfriend. . .

"Hi!" I called and waved to Nell, in case she didn't see me in the tucked-away corner of the Parade Café.

Out of habit, I touched the lapel of my jacket,

to show where my gold heart badge was. Nell half-heartedly waved back, but didn't make any gesture to show where *her* badge was pinned.

She didn't look quite like herself somehow; something was missing. Her smile? Her energy? The bright white light I always imagined radiating around her?

"Thought you'd be outside," said Nell as she sat down, nodding her head in the direction of the pavement tables in the bright sunlight.

"Didn't fancy it," I replied, preferring gloom, to match my mood.

It was Sunday morning, and the only people strolling around were those heading to Mr Patel's next door for morning papers, but that *still* felt like too many people to me. I mean, none of Mr Patel's customers would be *remotely* interested in me or Nell, or have a clue what our conversation would be about, but whatever. . . I *knew* I'd still imagine them staring, same as the party guests had done yesterday afternoon, once they'd realized something decidedly *strange* was going on.

"I think we'd better carry this on inside. . ." Dad had said, leading the way to the living room, looking ridiculous with his tongs and knitted apron now that our world had just turned inside out.

Between two sets of parents, there were blustered words, bits of explanation, blurred apologies . . . then it was hastily decided by someone (I forget who) that this conversation might have to be continued at a different time and at a different venue, since there was a garden full of confused guests, and two pretty shocked daughters on hand.

The conversation was carrying on now, this morning, without us, at Nell's house. I guess the McKenzie-Lee do-it-yourself knitted home was too frivolous a venue for such serious discussions. And it seemed as if all four of our parents thought that emotional thirteen-year-old daughters might just complicate the issue.

"So . . . what happened with the party?" asked Nell, opening the bottle of apple juice I'd already bought for her. I'd also bought her a Danish pastry (Mum and Dad had been generous with the cash, since they knew that while *they* were busy, me and Nell were getting together for our own private meeting).

Nell made no move to eat the pastry. The strangeness of the situation had obviously made her lose her appetite. I was the complete *opposite*: I was eating everything in sight, as if filling myself up would leave no room for the weird confusion of feelings that was trying to crush me.

"It carried on for a little while," I told her, thinking that my family might get in the record books for hosting the world's shortest party *ever*. "Dad went back out and tried to be sociable and forced everyone to have the burgers he'd made, but me and Mum were holed up in my room."

Yeah, me and Mum were in my room, with Mum desperately trying to explain.

Explain about meeting "John" when she was at a campsite in Death Valley (mmm, romantic name!), USA, when she was twenty-two.

How she and "John" fell slam-bang in love, and spent three blissful weeks camping and sightseeing round California together.

How they shipped up in tacky Las Vegas, Nevada for a day (just to check out how tacky it was), and somehow ended up thinking it was a fantastic idea to a) each get a tattoo with the other one's name on it from one of Las Vegas's many tattoo parlours (pity they chose the worst one), and b) get married in one of Las Vegas's many quickie wedding chapels (theirs was called The Eternal Love Chapel – ha!).

How – in the cold light of day – they both realized they'd made a *huuuuggggeee* mistake. How they decided they should part company, but meet up again in Britain to talk about things at the end of their travels.

How "John" left in a huff, without leaving "Belinda" any details of how to contact him.

How Mum felt ridiculously stupid for mistaking a nice but short-lived crush for true love, and tried to pretend to herself it never happened.

The end.

Until *yesterday*, that is. . .

And so, once everyone had tactfully sloped off from our failing party, it was *Dad's* turn to be alone with Mum in *their* room, listening to the same explanations that *I'd* just heard.

Next, all *three* of us were in the living room, going over everything again, but in the end I pleaded off with a thundering headache and went to bed at quarter to eight, sure that I had a night of non-sleeping ahead of me. Ha – I conked out the second I lay down, drugged by misery, and didn't wake up till gone nine this morning. Yeah, when I proceeded to eat every leftover piece of party food I could find.

(Mmm, stale popcorn. . .)

"So . . . how are you doing?" I asked my best friend, ready for some mutual sympathizing, now that we'd discovered Bibi and John's deep, dark, wedded secret.

Nell didn't so much answer as shrug.

Maybe she couldn't quite put it into words; the fact that our supposedly cool and fantastic and trustworthy parents had decided never to tell us – their beloved daughters – something pretty majorly important.

Never mind; I filled the vacuum with another question.

"Hey, my mum said that your dad had a tattoo as well? One that said 'I ♥ Bel—'"

"He got it removed years ago," Nell interrupted bluntly. "I remember always seeing a sort of white mark on his shoulder, but he once told me it was from an accident."

"An accidental marriage?" I tried to joke blackly.

Nell didn't laugh – she just gave another shrug. It kind of unnerved me.

I suddenly wanted to say a certain Something; a Something that might make her feel better . . . but then again, I was worried it might freak her out. I decided to keep the Something to myself for now, just till I figured out what was going on with Nell.

"So, how's *your* dad with the news?" Nell asked me, taking the tiniest, practically non-existent sip from her bottle.

Wow, she seemed so still and tense, and so . . . so *distant* from me. I wanted to put my arm around her, but I was scared that might make her cry. Actually, I'd have loved her to give me a what-a-mess hug too, but I couldn't exactly ask.

"My dad is . . ."

I thought for a second. He'd been furiously quiet and white-faced and mad-haired yesterday, from running his hands through it every five seconds as if he had a nervous tic. He just couldn't understand why Mum had never mentioned that she'd once been married, even if it *had* only been for half a second about a hundred years ago.

". . . sort of OK this morning."

Actually, now I thought about it, Dad was *remarkably* OK today. No jokes, no smiles, but not rigid with anger and bewilderment either. Wish *I* felt that way.

I stuffed another torn chunk of pastry in my mouth.

"What about your mum?" I asked her, spitting crumbs out unattractively with my question.

"She cried a bit – well, a *lot* on the way home yesterday. I mean, even though they'd never told me, Mum always knew Dad had . . . a . . . well, *wife* somewhere. Anyway, she said she was crying just from the shock of seeing your mother."

I didn't really *love* the way she said that, as if my mum was someone to be *shocked* by. As if Marianne couldn't believe that "her" John could be married to someone like Bibi, of all people.

But I was being stupid, and my nerves were raw. Nell didn't mean anything like that at all.

"She's better today, but she was a bit quiet before I left," Nell continued, talking to the neck of the bottle rather than directly to me. "I think that's 'cause she was completely dreading your parents coming around, though."

Hmmmm . . . Nell might not have meant anything by that either, but it wasn't a sentence that could be described as *tactful*.

"Well, I guess it was a little bit easier for your mum than my dad, since she at least knew that your dad was once married!" I said, as a suggestion, not an accusation.

Guess which way Nell took it?

"Hey, it was hardly *great* for her, knowing that Dad was married to someone who he couldn't divorce, 'cause his *wife* never got in touch!"

"But wait a minute: yesterday, your dad said *he* lost *her* details when he left his backpack on a Greyhound bus!"

"So you're saying it's *his* fault?" said Nell, looking animated at last – but not in a good way.

"Well, *sort* of – I mean, your dad went and left Las Vegas without giving my mum his home address or phone number or anything!"

"Yeah, but Dad said he wrote to her once he got to Texas; he sent her a letter care of the next campsite they were meant to have been going to in New Mexico!"

"But she didn't go there! She told me she was so upset after the wedding that she changed her mind and went to meet up with some backpacking friends who were in Cuba!"

"*She* was so upset! Yeah, *right*!" snapped Nell, her dark eyes flashing at me. "That's not exactly *true*, is it, since your *mother* was the one who wanted to call the whole thing off! Dad said *he* would've given it a chance!"

"So you're saying this is all my *mum's* fault?" I said, shaking like I hadn't eaten anything for days. Ha.

"Well, of *course* it is!" Nell said, wrinkling her nose and her face in what looked like disgust.

I thought about the Something I'd wanted to say to Nell a minute ago; I certainly didn't want to say it now.

All I wanted to do was *go*, before the raw edges of my nerves could be scuffed and scraped even *more* raw.

And so I went.

I hoped Nell might call after me, but she didn't. I hoped she might follow me out of the café, but she didn't. I dived into Mr Patel's shop, half-expecting to see her pass the window in a second, gazing frantically around for me, but that didn't happen.

What happened was, I found myself staring at some dumb celebrity style mags – the ones Tara used to buy (probably *still* bought) – just along the aisle from someone I knew. Well, *sort* of knew. Glen the *Big Issue* guy must've been off-duty; I certainly couldn't see any sign of his mag-stuffed bag, and it was Sunday after all, and probably his day off. He was leafing through some of the Sunday papers, while over by the counter, Mr Patel was cutting through the plastic cord of *another* bundle of papers to stack on the shelves.

I wasn't thinking about Secret Number Three (Glen's), or Secret Number Four (Mr Patel's), in case you were wondering. I was too busy burning up with rage at my mum for goofing up her life and ours; at my dad for seeming almost laid-back about the situation this morning; and at Nell's barbed words just now to care one minuscule *bit* about anything to do with the Karma Club.

I was a raging red being, with spikes of blinding gold jagging out.

Gold. . .

It triggered something in my head.

I'd ended up with the gold gel pen the other day, along with the stupid Karma Club notebook, which was in the slouch bag I had strapped across me. I slid my hand in, scrabbled around, and found it.

I don't know what made me do it; maybe the teen American actress grinning out of the cover of *Heat* didn't help. I resented her perfect life and her perfect career, and even her perfect, plastic-looking teeth. They weren't perfect for much *longer*. . .

I put the top back on the pen and slid it into the bag. I walked up to the counter, smiled at Mrs Patel, and took my time choosing the chocolate bar I wanted. I was just on my way out when I heard it; the thing that jarred me back into reality, out of my stupid red-tinged, gold-edged rage.

"Oi! What is this! Is *this* how you repay my kindness?!" Mr Patel yelled at Glen, waving a copy of *Heat* at him.

"But I didn't—!" I heard Glen start to protest, as I slunk out of the *blee*-bleeping shop door.

Oops.

Whether I'd meant it or not, the gold-teeth graffiti – on seven copies of the magazine, if Mr Patel cared to

count – was the Fourteenth Secret of the Karma Club.
And it was a very, very *bad* secret.

And as for the Something I'd meant to say to Nell?
Well, it was this: if things had worked out differently,
we might (possibly, *weirdly*) have been sisters.

Which was pretty funny, really; it really was.

If I'd felt like laughing, instead of crying. . .

The Fifteenth Secret

"Look, Kezzy, when you think about it, it's just not worth stressing about."

What?! The *more* I tried the uncomfortable business of thinking, the *more* reasons there seemed to get stressed out.

And I wasn't in the mood to be patronized as if *I* was the silly schoolgirl and *she* was the mature, intelligent adult.

Excuse me, but *which* of us had got married on a whim to someone they didn't really know very well and kept it secret for seventeen years?

Huh?!

I so badly wanted to say all that – *shout* all that at Mum, but it's very hard to say anything above a whisper in a crowded doctors' surgery without every germ-ridden person listening in. And while I was absolutely furious with her, I didn't want any more of the general public knowing the shameful details of my family's private life. It was bad enough that everyone at Saturday's lousy party was in on the hot gossip.

"*Mum,*" I hissed at her, flicking angrily and unseeingly through pages of the first crummy magazine I could lay my hands on when we came in here. "*Why* isn't it worth stressing about?"

I'd spent the whole day at school in a total haze of stress, from Monday-morning assembly to this very moment, when I'd come – as I'd promised last week, when I still thought my mum was amazing and sane – to her regular bump check-up at the doctors' surgery.

Who knew what Nell's stress levels were like? She hadn't even turned up at school today. Not that I cared. Much.

"It's not worth stressing about, because it's sorted, isn't it?" Mum said in an annoyingly calm, almost sing-songy kids'-TV-presenter voice. She seemed to be mistaking our lives for an episode of *Fifi and the Flowertots*.

"Oh, it's *sorted*, is it. Well that's *fine*, then, isn't it?" I muttered sarcastically, through gritted teeth. "You were secretly married to my best friend's dad. No problem. Hardly worth mentioning, really. Stupid of me to be bothered."

I shouldn't have come along. I should've just texted Mum and said I'd see her at home. I know I'd gone with her to every hospital or doctor's appointment I could so far, but today, I really couldn't concentrate on her *or* the bump. I was shrouded in a vapour of red rage again.

(*Don't think about Glen and Mr Patel falling out over my graffiti*, I warned myself, trying to keep from adding a dollop of guilt to my misery.)

"Honey, you know I *hate* that you're so upset! I wish I could say or do something to make it better for you!" Mum said heatedly, wrapping her arms around me in a mommy bear hug. Maybe people would think I was horribly ill and she was taking care of me. Ha. I'd never felt less taken care of in my life. Mum had managed to mess up a perfectly nice family *and* help lose me my new best mate, all in one go.

The only way she could make things any better was if she could assure me that she and Nell's dad had just made up the whole marriage mess as a bizarre elaborate joke. I *wish*. . .

"Gee, *thanks*," I answered her, bitterly, flatly.

"But, Kezzy, like I tried to explain to you yesterday, if your dad and I and John and Marianne have managed to talk it through and be all right with it, then *you* should feel . . . I don't know, *reassured* by that, I hope."

"Well, I'm sorry, but I don't feel too reassured."

"Honey, it's going to be all right! John and I will get solicitors to sort it out, and we'll get a divorce sorted out really, really quickly."

"Like *how* quickly?" I asked, staring intently at some ad for tooth-whitening paste in the dog-eared magazine. It might as *well* have been a magazine for dogs, for all the attention I was paying to it. *Elle Chien*, maybe. . .

"Well, as soon as we can, I guess," Mum answered breezily and vaguely. "As I said to John and Marianne, I'd prefer to leave all that complicated paperwork stuff till after the baby's born. I mean, that's only four more weeks, isn't it? Plus there'll be a while after when my brain will be too mushy to think of anything sensible, I suppose. . ."

She went thoughtful and quiet, taking my matching silence to be a good sign, I think, when *really* it was a sign that I was ready to explode and was trying very,

very hard indeed to not to stand up, scream and run out of the place.

Actually, if I didn't do the screaming or running bit. . .

"I need some fresh air. Back in a minute," I told her, without a backwards glance.

"Of course, honey! See you in a minute!" said Mum, unaware of the fact that my estimate was going to be out by about, ooh, seventeen *hours*. . .

I'd wanted to be with someone who'd known me – and my family – for years. I needed a familiar face, a familiar place, so I could stop feeling lost, for a little while at least.

But the problem was, I didn't recognize where I was, or who I was with.

Blinking around, I remembered the walls being powdery pink . . . but now they were a vivid purple, with silver, wine and green lines painted vertically down them, a cluster of stripes on each wall. It was bit like being on the inside of a gift-wrapped present.

And no pigs (but I should've expected that, after what Mum's friend Sheila had told me). The room looked bigger without large or small, smooth or fluffy, pottery or painted piggies cluttering up every surface. Actually, the only clutter was a couple of magazines (celeb stuff), a sleek silver hairdryer (with a complicated-looking diffuser attachment thing), and a whole bunch of make-up (were they allowed to wear that stuff at Brookfield School?).

The girl formerly known as my best friend Tara was

sitting on the edge of her bed, her hand splayed on her spectacular new bedside table, painting her nails fuchsia pink.

"Oh, hi, Kezzy," said Tara, giving me the most minimal of glances, and barely half a smile of welcome. She was trying to act like she'd seen me only yesterday; that it was no biggie me being here, though she *must* have heard her mum calling up the stairs just now to let her know I was – surprise, surprise – here to see her.

"Hey, Tara. . ." I answered, feeling my heart pounding at the strangeness of being here again after all this time. "How are you doing?"

I saw that she'd changed out of her newish school uniform (black blazer with a wine tartan skirt) and was lounging in black, velvety hip-hugging jogging bottoms and a skinny pink T-shirt. Her growing-out bob was struggling to stay in the ponytail she'd scraped it back into, though the overgrown fringe acted like a curtain to hide behind.

"Yeah, y'know. . ." she yawned theatrically.

Wow, it must be hard work pretending to be cool all the time.

Was I doing the right thing, coming here to talk to her today?

Too late – I was here now. What would I say if I suddenly tried to leave? "Oops! Meant to go to the library, but must have taken a wrong turn. Don't you just *hate* it when that happens?"

Aha – I could semi-see her reflection in the mirrored table. She was blinking fast, a giveaway to the fact that she wasn't as laid-back as she was pretending to be.

"So . . . what's going on with *you*?" Tara asked, feigning a whole skip-load of indifference, as she temporarily rested the bottle-top-'n'-brush back in the varnish bottle and inspected her first finished hand.

She was completely *desperate* to know why I was here, I could tell. I think a lot of the coolness was due to the fact that she was worried I'd come to give her a hard time about her birthday last week. Y'know, the *why-didn't-you-invite-me-too?* plea.

Like that mattered *one* little bit.

Her mother – Mrs Dixon – was dying to know too; she was hovering outside the slightly open bedroom door, I was certain. She used to do that all the time when me and Tara were friends. What was she expecting to hear? Us planning an armed robbery? Discussing how we could run away to join rebel insurgents in Colombia? Tara would hear the telltale creak of a floorboard and shout to her mother to leave us alone, before slamming the door shut.

"Something's happened," I said now, leaning myself up against her new mirrored chest of drawers, since I hadn't been asked to sit down.

The chest of drawers was amazing, and the matching bedside table too. They must have cost a *fortune* (a mega-birthday-present from Mr and Mrs Dixon?). If I hadn't had a deep, dark secret eating me up, I'd have spent a good long while cooing and drooling over this stuff. As it was, all I was doing was leaving sweaty palm prints on the pristine, polished surface.

"Oh? What *sort* of something?" asked Tara, finally stopping what she was doing and giving me her full attention. (The creaking on the landing stopped dead too, as Mrs Dixon paused to hear all.)

I let my eyes dart to the door, automatically slipping into the silent code we used to use when one of us sussed the presence of Mrs Dixon and her satellite-dish ears.

Looked like Tara spoke another language now; she didn't register my coded glance at all. Not a flicker.

Should I carry on? I couldn't *not*. I had to tell *someone*.

"You know my friend?" I continued, letting my fingers drum anxiously behind me on the mirrored chest of drawers. "The girl you've seen me with in the park? Nell?"

"Oh, yeah – the one with the frizzy dark hair?"

"Curly, yeah," I corrected, thinking I could so easily describe Robyn as the friend with the sulky face.

"Yeah, curly, whatever. . ." said Tara, dismissively waving a hand of fuchsia'd nails. "But what's happened?"

I should've stopped there, if I'd had any sense, but the shock of the last couple of days had zapped any semblance of sense right out of my fuzzy, non-functioning brain.

"I just found out that my mum is married to Nell's dad."

The "cool" practically dribbled out of Tara's mouth as it fell open. She looked gormless. I quite liked that.

Outside in the hall, I heard a distinct *thunk*, as Mrs Dixon hopefully fainted in shock and hit her head on a blunt object. Actually, she'd probably just bumped into something. (Hope it hurt.)

I shouldn't have come here, I really shouldn't. I think I'd been hoping for an instant hug and boundless sympathy, for old time's sake. But Tara was just staring at me as if I'd announced that I was here to set her house on fire.

"*What?*" she managed to squawk.

And so I told her, 'cause I didn't know how to get out of telling her now I'd come this far. It felt so strange to say all the facts out loud, instead of having them rattling noisily around my head like pinballs with no holes to disappear into.

"That is *so* sick!" Tara announced, as I finished with the stupidly civil parental summit yesterday and the plans to get divorce proceedings started, y'know, sometime, whenever, when Bibi and John could be bothered. . .

"I don't know about *sick*, but it is all deeply, *deeply* weird," I said, with a prickle of resentment. What Tara had just come out with, it sort of reminded me of that day in the park; the day of the First Secret, when she'd seen how pregnant Mum was getting and stared at her in barely disguised horror.

"Nah – it's totally *sick!*" Tara exclaimed, rocking on her bed and starting to laugh.

Laugh?! Was she crazy? Why was she finding this horrible situation so funny? 'Cause it wasn't happening to *her*? She was *sooo* shallow.

The intro to Gwen Stefani's "Hollaback Girl" trilled from a small, silver backpack at my feet.

"Oh, hold on . . . got to get that – could be important," Tara panted, sliding on to her knees, her unpainted hand slipping around in her bag as she tried to locate her mobile.

What? More important than the life-shifting news we were just talking about? Was she expecting a call from the prime minister or something?

"Hey, Robyn!" Tara grinned at my feet, her face all alert and alive, the way it most definitely *wasn't* when I'd walked in here.

Not really sure what to do, I switched places with her, stepping across the polished floorboards and sitting myself down on her bed, by the small mirrored bedside table.

"Nope. Nah . . . yeah? Ha ha ha!" chirped Tara, as I sat feeling smaller and smaller and dumber and dumber.

While I waited for Tara to finish her call, I stared at the semi-open bottle of nail varnish, and vaguely noticed that it was opaque, a thick, rich gloop of pink that suddenly reminded me of eating melty, coloured icing sugar meant for fairy cakes with my finger. I felt sick, even though I hadn't done that for years.

"Anyway, shut up, 'cause I've got *the* funniest thing to tell you!" said Tara, shooting me a *wait-for-this!* look.

Wait for what? To be humiliated?

"You know Kezzy? Yeah . . . yeah, *her*. Well, you'll never *guess* what she just found out about her mum. . ."

As she spoke, Tara distractedly doodled her index finger on the nearest polished floorboard, lost in her gossip.

Strangely enough, I found myself doodling my finger

over the top of her new mirrored table – and flicking the bottle of nail varnish over.

". . . so get this: it turns out SHE'S married to . . ."

"I've got to go," I muttered, getting up and striding across Tara's splayed legs.

My very-much-ex-best-friend gazed up at me in puzzlement, but made no attempt to stop me.

"Yeah, OK – bye!" she called out unfazed, as I hurtled from the bedroom, past Mrs Dixon listening in on the first-floor landing, down the stairs and out of the front door.

As I took giant steps away from the house, I felt a certain warm, defiant glow of pleasure at the thought of Tara discovering the Fifteenth (Sticky) Secret of the (Bad) Karma Club whenever she'd finished entertaining her mate with my misery.

But then the pleasure went on hold at the sound of my mobile's ringtone. I stopped dead, checking the screen for the caller ID.

Would it be Tara apologizing for being so thoughtless and unsympathetic?

Nell apologizing for being so horrible about my mum?

Mum apologizing for messing up our lives so badly?

Uh . . . no. It was Dad.

"Yep?" I said stiffly, ready for a very possible *where-are-you?-your-mum's-been-worried!* rebuke.

"Kezzy – you've got to come quick!"

Uh-oh. Could a couple of bad deeds add up to some kind of *serious* bad karma. . .?

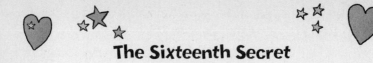

The Sixteenth Secret

Being born four weeks early isn't fantastic for a baby, but it's normally not too terrible either.

The drama surrounding the birth of my sister was 'cause. . .

a) she didn't seem very interested in *breathing* when she first popped into the world, and . . .

b) Mum's body apparently thought it might be a fun idea to haemorrhage lots of blood right after the birth and make the medical staff panic madly.

So although my sister arrived startlingly quickly – only two hours after I left Mum in the doctors' surgery, and her waters unexpectedly broke – all the chaos afterwards meant that I didn't get to see them till eleven-thirty the next morning, i.e., seventeen hours after Mum had called out, "Of course, honey! See you in a minute!"

"Ready?" asked Dad, as we walked down the long white corridor, our trainers squeaking on the scuffed vinyl flooring.

Gran and Grandad, who'd sped (literally) down from Leeds last night to look after me, were hovering downstairs in the hospital canteen. It wasn't proper visiting hours yet, but I was being allowed in to see Mum, due to the circumstances (i.e., the fact that she'd nearly – gulp – died, and was desperate to see me).

"Uh, yep!" I replied with a wibble in my voice, choked up with excitement and relief and who knows what else. (*Guilt*, actually. I shouldn't have left Mum yesterday when she needed me. Or at least when she was just *about* to need me.)

"Then let's go see your little sis!" Dad said with a smile, looking tired and drawn and unshaven and ecstatic.

He was doing OK, though, for someone who'd been up all night, half-prepared for both Mum and the baby not to make it.

Luckily (for me), I'd finally fallen into a tossy-turny sleep at the time when everything seemed at its most black. And I'd woken up with the first light of dawn, oblivious to the fact that things were looking amazingly, thankfully brighter for both Mum and the baby by then.

I'm glad in a way that I didn't know all that stuff. That kind of secret is good, when the truth could drive you crazy with worry.

But right now I had someone special to meet. I clutched the knitted tomato baby hat and matching all-in-one that I'd brought from home and braced myself.

"Here goes," murmured Dad, as he pushed a blue door open to a small ward. There were three beds visible . . . one empty, two filled with women I didn't know, and one bed hidden behind a garishly patterned curtain.

Nervously, I peeked around the curtain – and tried not to panic at the sight of Mum lying back on a mound of pillows, her skin paper-white and practically transparent, tubes and wires stuck into the back of her hand and who knows where else.

"Kezzy, baby!" she crooned to me, lifting her arms up weakly for a hug.

I think I probably squeezed her too hard, but she didn't seem to mind. Still, I let her go – she seemed very breakable at the moment and I needed her in one piece, never mind the baby.

Speaking of which. . .

"What do you think?" asked Mum, nodding her head at the clear plastic box on wheels parked by the side of her bed.

It was hard to hear Mum; her voice was as weak as *she* was and the baby was yelling in a small, thin but *furious* wail. The Cute Ugly Barky Dog was going to have competition in our street over who was the loudest, *that* was for sure.

I bent over and studied this perfectly gorgeous, perfectly tiny, perfectly prawn-red howling creature. She was like a living, breathing science experiment. I'd never seen anything so amazing. And I'd never seen nails that minuscule. . .

"What are we calling her?" I asked, almost sensing a hint of a grin when I thought of Nell's long-ago suggestion of Screaming Blob. It would suit my baby sister perfectly for now, but maybe it wouldn't be so good later, if she became an accountant or a dentist or president of the United Nations or something.

"Well, your dad and I are kind of stuck. . ." said Mum, wincing a little with the effort of playing name-the-baby (or maybe it was in pain, of course). "We've been looking at her this morning and thinking maybe Clara? Or Florence?"

"But we're not sure," Dad added, leaning over to stroke the baby's tiny, frowning, beetroot-red forehead with the back of his pinkie. It didn't soothe her.

I stared down at my sister . . . Clara? Florence?

I'm sorry, I don't think so, I thought to myself, feeling a wave of big sister protectiveness wash over me. Clara and Florence were perfectly cute, but not for *this* little madam.

Oh, no. *I* knew a name that would suit her *right* down to the ground. . .

My sister has arrived early. It was all a bit scary. Her name is Scarlet Amelie McKenzie. See you later? K x

Scarlet for the furious red of her skin when she bawled, and Amelie for the magical ray of sunshine she'd blasted into our family at *just* the right time.

"Who are you texting, love? One of your friends?" Granny turned and smiled at me over the back of her car seat on the way to school.

My grandparents were dropping me back in time for the afternoon session. Dad was staying at the hospital a bit longer, so he could speak to the doctors about how Mum and Scarlet were doing and how long they'd have to stay in for. Though how he'd be able to listen to what the doctors were saying when he was asleep on his feet was anyone's guess.

"Uh . . . yeah, it's my, um, friend from school," I found myself explaining, editing out the "best" bit from the "friend" bit, since I couldn't say that's what we were any more. To be honest, I didn't think we could even be described as friends these days, but that was *way* too complicated to explain on a day when we were all tired and emotional.

I guess it was 'cause I felt emotional that I'd decided to text Nell; plus I didn't want to walk into class this afternoon and see her cold, with thoughts of Sunday's arguments in our heads. *If* she was back, that was – she was off school yesterday, wasn't she? Suffering from a bad case of don't-want-to-be-near-Kezzy-itis, maybe. . .

Grandad's Vauxhall Vectra was stuck behind a bus, very near the row of shops, when I got her reply. My heart missed a beat or three at the sight of her name on the screen . . . and went into freefall when I read the flat, emotion-free message.

Congratulations. Won't be back at school till Monday – got a virus.

No warmth, no chattiness, no initial signing off, no kiss.

"Grandad! Can you drop me here? I can walk to school in plenty of time!" I said hastily, with a sudden urge to sort something out. I didn't know quite *how* I was going to do that yet, but it wasn't going to come to me sitting here in this car, wedged between two buses.

"But it's easy enough for us to drive you right there, Kezzy, love!" Gran protested.

"No, it's fine! I just want to . . ." I glanced around for

inspiration, spotting first Glen the *Big Issue* guy – who was pointedly standing outside the chemist's – then Mr Patel's shop, of course. ". . . I want to go and buy a baby card for Mum and Dad."

With an understanding, "Aw, isn't that sweet?" and kisses and promises to pick me up from school later, my grandparents let me go, as the bus and cars stuck behind the Vectra honked for them to move.

In a gap in the traffic, I zipped across, hearing – before I saw – a certain neighbour of mine.

"Hello there!" I said to the Cute Ugly Barky Dog, whose lead was tied around a chair outside the Parade Café. He rewarded me with silence and an appreciative wet lick.

"Oh, hello!" said the bland-looking bald man, weaving between tables and chairs with a cup of coffee in his hand. "Admiring his new collar, are you?"

"I hadn't noticed!" I replied, noticing now. It was a shiny patent red, with fake rhinestones. It was so tacky it was excellent. "It's good!"

"Well, over the last few days, Buddy's had a *lot* of attention from that woolly ribbon thing that someone put on him – but then he ate it. Still, I decided to get him something fun again, so little kids wouldn't be scared of him, you know?"

I knew. And I felt very pleased that the Twelfth Secret had worked so well. Then I caught myself glancing along the row of shops at Glen and wishing I hadn't messed up so badly with Secrets Three and Four.

"Um, by the way . . . everything OK with your parents now?" the bland, bald guy asked gingerly.

"Yeah, brilliant – Mum had the baby last night!" I said gushingly. "Her name's Scarlet. I'm just going to go and get her and Dad a card."

"Ah . . . great. I'll pop one through the door myself later."

It was only once I'd said bye and gone into Mr Patel's that I realized what the bland, bald guy had really meant; he was talking about the showdown with Nell's parents at the barbecue on Saturday. I'd been thinking about Mum and the baby so much that I'd somehow managed to totally forget the big argument.

Well, hey, maybe little Scarlet Amelie would work her magic on all the friends and neighbours like she did on our family and use her very existence to eclipse all the mad, bad stuff.

And now I had some eclipsing of my own to do.

"That'll be £2.50, please," said Mrs Patel, as she carefully put my six postcards in a pretty, flowery paper bag. The postcards had corny photos of woodland creatures on them, which was pretty bizarre since there weren't exactly a lot of roe deer and red squirrels in the middle of the city where we were. Still, what was on them wasn't the point; it was what was *going* to be on them that was important.

"Oh, and seven stamps, please," I said, blowing a big hole in my pocket money (hey, Mum and Dad would probably prefer a home-made card anyway).

"Don't you want just six?" asked Mrs Patel. "You only have six postcards. . ."

"No, seven stamps; that's fine," I assured her. The truth was, I needed to buy one more postcard, but it couldn't be from this shop, or Mr Patel (who'd be receiving it) would recognize it and maybe figure out it came from me.

Speaking of Mr Patel, he was at the other end of the counter from the till, and was doing some kind of accounts. He had that angry, vivid red glow to him again; the glow I recognized from having it hanging round me like a shroud the last couple of days. But the only red I wanted to see in my life from now on was a little girl called Scarlet.

"There we go!" said Mrs Patel brightly, handing me my bag and my change.

Little did she know that the innocent-looking postcards and stamps inside the paper bag were actually the Sixteenth Secret.

Otherwise known as my personal secret weapon – to help right the wrongs that had been happening way too often lately. . .

A Break From Secrets
(Apart From the Big Secret
of the Universe)

I might not have mentioned it, but I can knit.

You can't really be the daughter of the punk goddess of knitting and avoid being taught how to knit one, purl one.

I just never really do it because a) I'm not that interested in it, and b) when you're related to someone who's a genius at knitting, nothing you do is ever going to be remotely as amazing as what *they* do, so it kind of puts you off. Well, it's always put *me* off.

But right now, I'd made a special effort, in honour of Mum.

It was a bit scrappy and uneven, but hopefully it was in her style.

"*ATTENTION REBEL KNITTERS*," I'd typed on the top of the A4 sheet of paper. "*There will be no meeting this Saturday, and until further notice, due to the early but safe arrival of SCARLET AMELIE! Bibi sends her love and hopes to see you all soon. . .*"

Mum had dictated the message to me yesterday evening during visiting hours (she and Scarlet had been kept in hospital all week, but were hopefully going to come home on Monday). As soon as I got home I'd printed it out on my computer – picking out "Scarlet" and "Amelie" in a bright red ink – and then raided Mum's knitting cupboard.

While Dad and Gran and Grandad had watched some Friday-night TV shows and tried to relax, I'd clicked and clacked, and dropped and picked up a few stitches until I'd made a long, lacy mauve ribbon thing that I'd then shaped into a frame to go around Mum's message.

"Looks good!" said Helen, the lady who ran the park café, as she set up the tables for the day, and checked out the message I was Blu-tacking to the door. "Send Bibi my love, won't you? Oh, and let me cut you some of this gorgeous lemon drizzle cake to take to her when you visit the hospital this afternoon. . ."

I followed Helen inside the shop, smiling when I thought of the strange mix of gifts I had to pass on to Mum today: apart from lemon drizzle cake (wow, those slices were big enough for everyone on Mum's ward to have a piece!), there was a miniature Fair Isle jumper made by rebel knitter Sheila (with stitches so small she must have been using fairy-sized needles), a hamper stuffed with nappies, baby creams and earplugs (a joke from Mum's work mates), a flowering cactus (from Buddy-the-dog's owner – I don't think a man living on his own with a dog really knows what to do when it comes to babies), and a CD of lullabies done in a reggae style (from one of Dad's friends).

"There you go!" smiled Helen, swivelling around and handing me a brown paper bag with lots of lemony drizzle-ness inside of it.

"Thanks!" I said, turning to go.

But I didn't get very far, as there was someone standing in the doorway, framed in bright, almost white sunshine.

The someone was smiling sort-of-shyly at me, and holding out a postcard.

I took the postcard, smiling just as shyly back at Nell. The picture side showed a corny-looking kitten sitting beside a corny-looking vase of flowers, but I knew straight away that it was the *other* side I was meant to be looking at.

"*YES.*"

That was all it said, and it was the *exact* word I'd hoped would be there.

"You got them, then?" I asked, mirroring what Nell was doing and sitting down at the nearest table.

"Uh-huh," Nell said with a nod, and a big, *wide* smile this time.

From her pocket, she took a bundle of postcards.

"I got this one –" *[a red squirrel]* "– and this one –" *[a badger]* "– on Thursday, but they didn't make any sense till this one –" *[a fox cub]* "– came yesterday, and these two –" *[a roe deer and an owl]* "– arrived in the post this morning."

Nell flipped them all over, to the side with her name and address on, and put them in order.

"'*PLEASE*' '*CAN*' '*WE*' '*FRIENDS*' '*BE*'?" I read out loud and laughed.

"Oops!" giggled Nell, hurriedly rearranging the last two postcards so that they read like a modern sentence and not like something out of Shakespeare.

It was a huge relief to know the cards had worked. There was no way I could know if the *other* two I'd sent had worked as well, but I'd just have to keep my fingers crossed . . . plus watch to see if Glen was back to standing in his old pitch, and if Mr Patel was letting him use his loo again.

Mind you, I'd sort of decided to avoid Mr Patel's and the row of shops for a while – till I was *sixteen*, maybe – in case Mr Patel or Glen sussed out that the postcards, and the apologies, came from *me*. I might have written them anonymously, but neither of them needed to have a brain like Inspector Closeau to think back and remember that I was in the shop last Sunday morning. . .

So what had I written to them? Well, on Mr Patel's card (a photo of the city square from the 1980s) I'd put, "*Hello. Last Sunday I scribbled gold teeth on some of your magazines. I am TRULY sorry for doing something so stupid. Love, K (aged 13)*". At the last minute, I'd taped on what was left of my pocket money (not enough to pay for *all* the magazines I'd damaged, but a gesture whatever), put the whole lot in an envelope and sent it off. On Glen's card I wrote, "*I was the one who graffiti'd on Mr Patel's magazines last Sunday – I've written and told him. I'm sorry that you got the blame. K (aged 13)*". I sent it care of the chemist's shop that Glen had been standing outside all week.

I'd tell Nell about the Fourteenth and the Sixteenth Secrets sometime, but maybe not right now, when we had other stuff on our minds, like sticking our friendship back together. And hey, she'd get a buzz from hearing about the Fifteenth Secret, I was sure.

Y'know, for half a second, I'd considered sending Tara a "sorry" postcard too, apologizing for the spilt varnish, but then I figured it wouldn't work, because it wouldn't be anonymous, and also – when I thought about it – I realized I didn't feel very sorry for doing it in the *first* place. Not nice, I know, but maybe Tara had brought on her *own* bad karma.

Look, I know it's a useless excuse, but I don't think karma is an exact science, er, exactly. . .

"Here, a treat from me. To say congratulations about your little sister," said Helen the café owner, suddenly plonking two cartons of juice down on our table.

"Thanks!" I mumbled bashfully after her, amazed at how lovely everyone had been since they heard the news about Scarlet.

"Oh, and this is from me," said Nell, reaching down into her bag and pulling something out – a gift-wrapped little parcel. "It's this padded sign thing to hang in Scarlet's room; it says '*100% Cute*', sewn on in sequins."

"Thanks!" I said, feeling myself go pink with happiness as she slid the present over towards me.

"Yeah, well, whatever . . . she'll probably *drool* all over it."

I guess Nell was joking around to cover up her own awkwardness, so I joined in too.

"Or *barf* all over it!"

"Yeah!" giggled Nell, reaching down towards her bag again. "And this card's for your parents, from mine."

I took it. Nell took a sip of her drink though her straw and studied me, to see what my reaction was, I suppose.

And my reaction was this: prickles of goosebumps all over. I mean, it seemed *weird* that Nell's parents would be giving Mum and Dad a card. If I let it, it might make me feel freaked out again, when I'd only just started to feel normal.

So I decided to risk fooling around again.

"That's nice. If any of the nurses ask who this is from, Mum can tell them it's from her husband – and his girlfriend!"

A slap in the face; that's what my "joke" could have felt like to Nell. Luckily, it made her choke instead; a shower of apple juice shot out of her nose as she struggled to laugh and breathe at the same time.

"So anyway, before Scarlet happened, my parents were acting like the whole 'oops-we're-married' thing was all no big deal," I began, launching into the tough subject at hand, once we'd stopped sniggering and found a serviette to clean up Nell and the table. "How about yours?"

"Yeah, Dad's been like that too, acting all laid-back and well-what's-done-is-done. Mum's *not* been so great," explained Nell, shrugging a little and fidgeting with the soggy serviette. "I mean, she's sort of getting *used* to the whole deal now, but she was pretty upset."

I suddenly remembered what Nell had said to me in the Parade Café, when everything went a bit . . . *spiky*. She'd told me that her dad had come out with something about how *he'd* have given the whole love and marriage thing a go, even if *my* mum hadn't been up for it. That must have been kind of *excruciating* for Nell's mum Marianne to hear, I guess.

"The other night, my mum told me that one of the toughest things was just meeting Bibi – she'd heard me waffle on about how amazing your mum was for ages, and then this vision of quirky coolness appears in front of her . . . and oops!, the amazing woman turns out to be married to my *dad*!"

Poor Marianne. Sounded like she was as freaked out about the whole thing as me and Nell. And Nell, I suppose, was really, *understandably*, protective of her mum.

"Are your parents OK now, though?" I asked, slipping back slightly into that "I think Mum might have ruined *everything*!" vibe.

"Yeah, pretty much. But I did panic a bit. I mean, we're always moving about and leaving people and places behind, and . . . and . . . for a second there I thought all this might make them . . . well . . . *y'know*."

Yeah, I knew; split up.

Nell's sentence trailed off uselessly, but I understood completely. Anyone meeting my lovely best friend for the first time would probably score her ten-out-of-ten for confidence, but *I'd* only just started to realize that she might be hiding a whole heap of wibbleness and worry inside, the second anything went wrong. (And *boy* does finding out that your dad is secretly married to your best friend's mum count as *wrong*.)

"Bibi and your dad: they're going to sort it out, though, and get a divorce really soon," I tried to reassure her.

"Yeah, but when?" Nell looked at me pleadingly. "Dad said they'd probably leave it for a while, and sort it when your parents weren't so busy with the baby. But when's *that* going to be?"

"Well, seeing as it's taken them seventeen years to tell us that they were both married in the first place – never mind to each other – I guess maybe Scarlet will be just about finishing university by the time they get round to finally divorcing!"

We looked at each other, me and Nell, knowing that was a funny remark, but knowing too that it might come true, if our annoyingly chilled-out parents (well, some of them) had anything to do with it.

"Hey, Kezzy – d'you think that maybe we need to think up some secret way of getting them to. . ."

Once again, Nell's sentence fizzled out. I think it's 'cause both of us were well and truly frazzled with secrets. We needed a break from them, even the most well-meaning, fantastically sparkly good ones.

"Nah. Me and you should just go home and tell Bibi and John that we want them to *do* it *now*," I said firmly, slapping my hand on the table. "No messing – my mum and your dad need to call some solicitor . . . people. . . whoever, *next* week, and get the whole divorce thing started."

Or whole marriage thing *ended*, more appropriately.

Nell beamed at me, as if I'd just told her the secret of life, or the recipe for Ben and Jerry's Phish Food ice cream.

There were pink splatches flaring up on my neck, I could feel, but that was OK. They were there because I wasn't usually any good at being strong and determined, and I'd gone a little shy on myself.

But here's the thing: I'd suddenly realized a Big Secret of the Universe, one that you don't tend to know till you get a bit older.

And it was this: ADULTS CAN BE USELESS, AND NOT KNOW WHAT THEY'RE DOING.

True fact. . .

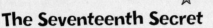

The Seventeenth Secret

I feel things in colour.

And the colour I was feeling at the moment was brown.

Brown, dandelion-clock soft mohair, the "tree" I once thought my mum might be knitting.

Turned out, the unknown brown thing was an oversized, slash-necked top that hung off one of my shoulders in a very cool way. It looked good with a vest top worn underneath, and over a pair of cut-off jeans and trainers. On the front, in swirly, gold-embroidered lettering, it read, *"You're looking at the big sister, OK?"* Down at the bottom, on the right, Mum had embroidered her name: *"Bibi Lee"*.

It had taken a while for her to finish it, since Scarlet had been so curious about us all that she'd arrived (rather spectacularly) early in the world, putting paid to knitting plans temporarily.

But as soon as Mum got her energy back, she threw herself into her pet hobby like a punk goddess of knitting reborn.

She'd made a weaving mill's worth of baby outfits for Scarlet (I liked the tiddly Tigger Babygro best, complete with ears and tail). She'd made personalized invitations for new members to join the Rebel Knitters' Society.

(Maybe Mrs Audrey Cooper, Sonia the once-Harassed Single Mum and Nell's mum Marianne could use them as dusters or tea towels afterwards. I should've suggested that last Saturday, at the Rebel Knitters' Society's first meeting since my sis complicated everything.)

By the way, in case you wanted to know, Audrey is knitting a very small scarf – very slowly, 'cause her broken wrist isn't what it used to be – but she seems very happy to be sitting and chatting in the late-summer sunshine with Mum and Mrs Laskaris and Sheila and Elzbieta and everyone. Sonia is trying her best to knit, but with Joe and her brood of little kids mooching around – playing in the paddling pool and then demanding her attention – it must be hard to concentrate on anything, except keeping up with the gossip around the table. Nell's mum Marianne is making a surprise birthday pressie for Nell's dad; an old-fashioned sampler with one of his wonky-type sayings on it: "*All's Well That Ends Well (Sort Of)*". Which seems pretty appropriate to me, anyway.

I guess everything *has* ended quite well.

Mum spent most of the last couple of months knitting wedding invitations to everyone, but that tied in nicely with the fact that she and John managed to get a very, very quick quickie divorce, since they'd been apart for so long.

Everyone who's had a knitted invitation is coming (well, who in their right mind could refuse a knitted invitation?). The lilac wool ones are for the actual wedding at the registrar's during the day; the avocado-green wool ones are for the party – i.e., the barbecue in our back garden – at night. Buddy the dog got his own avocado-green invite, and has RSVP'd (along with his owner) with a "woof!", which we think means yes.

I told Miss Lennard about my parents (finally) getting married when I bumped into her out of school. I *had* to say something; I'd caught her looking at me a bit strangely, since at the time, I was buying up Mr Patel's entire stock of dusty old boxes of confetti. (Glen had just excuse me'd his way past to go to the loo in the back of the shop.)

Miss Lennard went a bit teary and happy when I explained, which made me feel pretty good (better than seeing her staring into space out of the school window, which I hadn't – thankfully – seen her do in the last couple of weeks before we broke up for the summer holidays).

Anyway, back to the wedding itself: Nell's mum and dad have RSVP'd to say yes please, which is just as well, as there are going to be three bridesmaids present when Neil Richard McKenzie gets himself hitched to Belinda (Bibi) Lee . . . and that's me, Scarlet (my baby sister) and Nell (who might, like I said, have been my sister, in a parallel universe).

But enough of all the slushy-gushy, lovey-dovey stuff, 'cause there's *one* more secret to own up to.

The Seventeenth Secret of the Karma Club.

And it's this: if Mum is thinking about *knitting* bridesmaids' dresses, I'm not kidding; however much I love her, I'm running away from home. . .

Meet the sparkly-gorgeous Karen McCombie!

⋆ **Describe yourself in five words. . .**

Scottish, confident, shy, calm, ditzy.

⋆ **How did you become an author-girl?**

When I was eight, my teacher Miss Thomson told me I should write a book one day. I forgot about that for (lots of) years, then when I was working on teen mags, I scribbled a few short stories for them and suddenly thought, "Hmmm, I'd love to try and write a book . . . can I?"

⋆ **Where do you write your books?**

In the loft room at the top of our house. I work v. hard 'cause I only have a little bit of book-writing time – the rest of the day I'm making Playdough dinosaurs or pretend "cafés" with my little daughter, Milly.

⋆ **What else do you get up to when you're not writing?**

Reading, watching DVDs, eating crisps, patting cats and belly dancing!

Want to know more. . .?

Join Karen's club NOW!

For behind-the-scenes gossip on Karen's very own blog, fab competitions and photogalleries, become a fan member now on:

www.karenmccombie.com

P.S. Don't forget to send your bezzie mate a gorge e-card once you've joined!

Karen says:

"It's sheeny and shiny, furry and er, funny in places! It's everything you could want from a website and a weeny bit more. . ."

Have you checked out *Sadie Rocks?* Books 1 and 2 are out now and *utterly brilliant* – don't miss them!